THE OTHER HALF OF ME

Also by Emily Franklin

Emily Franklin

THE OTHER HALF OF ME

Delacorte Press

ACKNOWLEDGMENTS

This book would not have been possible without Claudia Gabel—thank you!

Also big thanks to Faye Bender, who deserves a trip to a fancy cooking school, like the Faye in this novel.

I revisited the art in this book because of Sam Strauss, who can tell Klee from Klimt and showed me, again, the magic of *The Starry Night,* but who mainly shows me the magic of being his mom.

Published by Delacorte Press
an imprint of Random House Children's Books
a division of Random House, Inc.
New York

www.randomhouse.com/teens

Educators and librarians, for a variety of teaching tools, visit us at
www.randomhouse.com/teachers

Library of Congress Cataloging-in-Publication Data
Franklin, Emily.
The other half of me / Emily Franklin. — 1st ed.
p. cm.
Summary: Feeling out of place in her athletic family, artistic sixteen-year-old Jenny Fitzgerald, whose biological father was a sperm donor, finds her half sister through the Sibling Donor Registry and contacts her, hoping that this will make her feel complete.
ISBN: 978-0-385-73445-5 (trade)
ISBN: 978-0-385-90449-0 (lib. bdg.)
[1. Identity—Fiction. 2. Brothers and sisters—Fiction. 3. Family life—Connecticut—Fiction. 4. Artists—Fiction. 5. Painting—Fiction. 6. Dating (Social customs)—Fiction. 7. Connecticut—Fiction.] I. Title.
PZ7.F8583Ot 2007
[Fic]—dc22
2006036825

The text of this book is set in 11-point Sabon.
Printed in the United States of America
10 9 8 7 6 5 4 3 2 1
First Edition

For my brothers

ONE

I am not alone. Of course I'm aware that those are words people tell themselves at precisely the moments in which they feel completely alone. But I'm trying to shrug that off as I stare at the blank wall in front of me and try to picture what should go there. Fine, so it's not an entire wall—it's a canvas on a wall in an art studio—and I have precisely twelve minutes to paint something before Sidney Sleethly, the director of Downtown Studios, kicks me out for the day so other, "real" artists (read: ones who sell things and therefore make him money) can take over my tiny space.

He likes to be called Sid because he worships punk rock icon Sid Vicious, but this man is a far cry from that kind of crazy-cool. In fact, the only reason I tolerate being tolerated by Sleethly is because his studio, with its cavernous rooms, floor-to-ceiling windows, and various walls on which to display art, is the only place I truly feel at home. Even if within that feeling of homeyness (a word I can't stand since it reminds me of needlepointed pillows and stale sugar cookies that look good but taste like crap) is a morsel of loneliness.

All in all, though, I'm not a lonely person, at least not in that crying, snot-on-the-sleeve, I-just-watched-some-parent-child-reunion-on-daytime-TV way. I'm just alone, as in unaccompanied for another ten minutes before I slog through the belt of late-summer rain to pick up my sisters from camp. After that I'll go back to my house, where it's impossible to be alone, and not only because of my sibling overload (twin sisters and a brother). The idea of personal space (not to mention personal freedom) isn't high on my parents' list of goals (and yes, there's an actual list on the fridge). Number three on the list—"Try until you get it right"—was added by my mom and dad after one of our theme dinners (this one was fajitas and virgin margaritas on the lawn, complete with a piñata my mother made in a fit of craftiness). Everyone (everyone includes me; my brother, Russ; my sisters, Sierra and Sage, aka the whiny twins; and my ultracheerful and khaki-loving parents) had to wear floppy sombreros and listen to lame mariachi music. The evening wouldn't have been so bad (in fact, the food my dad cooked was pretty tasty) if only I hadn't had to deal with batting at the piñata.

Unlike the rest of the Fitzgerald clan, I am not, as they say, athletically inclined. Or as my gym teacher commented to my mother, "Jenny's lack of skill is only outdone by her lack of enthusiasm in class." Basically, if there's a field, a ball, and an implement with which to hit that ball, I suck. Russ (short for Russet—he's two years younger, but way ahead of me in the high school social sphere with his cool jocky friends and sporting talent) hit the fish-shaped piñata blindfolded and backward. Sierra and Sage, their long straight hair swinging in graceful ponytails, whacked the thing until it nearly burst. My parents hit it no problem, and just when you could see the candy poking out from inside, it was my turn. I knew everyone had tried to prep the piñata for me, making it so easy I couldn't fail.

And yet I did. No matter how long I stood there, I couldn't make the bat connect with the papier-mâché fish. I couldn't make the candy spill out. I couldn't be what everyone wanted me to be: another sporty, varsity-playing Fitzgerald. With all due respect, I am the *I* in *team*. After the piñata incident, I wasn't that surprised to see the addition of "Try until you get it right" on the list of family goals taped to the fridge.

I'm centered enough not to fall apart over seeing that on the list, even though it was added right after I stormed out of the family fun with the piñata still relatively intact. I watched from my bedroom as Sierra spun Sage around until she could hardly stay upright and yet managed to aim the bat perfectly at the mangled fish, bonking it only once, to cause a shower of rainbow-colored candies to fall on our green lawn.

Maybe that's what I should paint now on the canvas. A green lawn with dots of pastel candies on it. It's kind of a cool image, a rain-wet lawn with splotches of colors, some hidden amid the grass. Or maybe I should draw something outside my suburban existence, some cityscape or a foreign country's teeming streets. I can't decide. Before thoughts of my crowded house get to me, I turn back to the canvas.

Blue? Blech. No one likes to look at blue art. It's too done, too easily readable.

What if I mix cerulean with light gray? I test out a couple of colors on my palette, which in this case is a recycled egg carton. Real palettes cost money, and the good one I have is kept in my closet at home. I figure I'll use it and the white-boar-bristle brushes I saved for but haven't tried out when I consider my work worthy, which at this point I don't. Not that my paintings are bad. This one is taking shape, sort of an arching design in muted colors that gives way to the bright hues I'm adding now. The indigo fuses with the deep red, which resembles the color of a certain boy's delicate-looking lips. I'm actually thinking that my work isn't totally awful, when . . .

"Dear Diary, Today I made a piece of art that looks as though a first grader got hold of my brush." Sid Sleethly's mocking voice disrupts my last few minutes of quiet, causing my paintbrush (and my ego) to slide down. He is notoriously obnoxious (the British accent only makes it worse), and this moment doesn't do anything to disprove that. Still, I've become accustomed to the way he acts. After climbing the ladder of art success in the 1980s in New York and then oozing back down, one is bound to have a severe attitude problem.

"Now look what you've done," I say under my breath, wiping off the spot where green has intruded into the red and blue.

"I'm only being honest with you. Isn't that what all artists want, brutal honesty?"

I like being classified with "all artists," but other than that, Sid's words get under my skin.

"I could do without the brutal part." I start to clean the brushes, dipping them in turpentine, which stings my nostrils and makes my eyes water. Or maybe that's just an emotional reaction to his comment. Granted, I know this particular painting isn't fantastic, but I'd like to think . . .

"You probably think that this work is"—Sid flings his hand in the general vicinity of my painting like he's trying to diffuse an unpleasant smell—"on its way to being something. But it's not."

Instead of arguing with him, I blush and clench my stomach muscles and mouth so as not to reveal anything. I don't have the time for arguing, anyway. My studio time is limited and my parents demand my presence at dinner, even now, in what's left of summer. I also have to shuttle my sisters from their day camp, so leaving now is key if I'm going to make it on time. Besides, I hate arguing in my defense. Part of me thinks that when everything works, it's without the aid of words. You're just supposed to know what's right, or what people need.

"Thanks for the advice, Sid," I say with enough sarcasm that I feel a bit better but not enough that he can call me on it.

"You *will* thank me one day, Jenny Fitzgerald. All art needs criticism in order to grow, and, well, yours might need extra since all it is right now is your vision of what you think other people want you to be." When he uses my full name like that, it drives home the fact that he hasn't

5

sold one of my paintings and that none of them really re-quires my signature at the bottom.

Without saying anything more, Sid (thankfully) leaves me in the mess of my paints and the muck of his harsh words, which feel particularly harsh today because of my suspicion that they're true.

Outside, the rain pelts my head, soaking my hair and my carefully selected not-too-tight white T-shirt. I can only imagine what I look like, and it can best be described as someone who belongs on the cover of a "men's interest" magazine. I cross my arms over my chest and wonder if I can just pull up at Camp Cedar and beep or if I have to ac-tually go inside and physically claim my sisters. Usually they get a ride with my mom, but in an attempt to encour-age my "family bonding time" (Mom's words, not mine), I have been enlisted as the twins' chauffeur.

Driving is pretty new to me still, so I automatically go through the list of what I'm supposed to do before backing up—put on seat belt, adjust rearview mirror, check side mirrors, and look for oncoming cars. All fine—that is, ex-cept for the glimpse of myself in the rearview mirror: my normally average hair (Russ says it's the color of toffee) is a shade darker and slicked to my face, and my nose is run-ning. Lovely.

I turn up the heat in the car in the hope it will dry my shirt by the time I get to Camp Cedar, which is all of eight minutes down the road on the far side of town (town being Cutler, Connecticut, your typical white-steepled New

England historic vale). Of course, the heat makes the windows fog, causing my hair to get that weird peach fuzz frizz on the top, and my shirt is no less wet than it was before.

Even though I want to be that artist girl who is so wrapped up in her paint box and deep thoughts that she doesn't think at all about her looks, I'm just not. However, I don't care *that* much. My clothes are splattered with various hues from my artistic renderings, and my hair doesn't change per the latest fashion mags, but I'm not oblivious to looking decent (or trying to), either.

For example, right now I care quite a bit how I appear. Not only do I have to snag Sierra and Sage from a bevy of preteen beauties, but I have to do so in front of a certain someone. A certain someone I can't look in the eye or admit to admiring, at least not out loud. There's a part of me that still believes if you say things out loud, it's as though you're not only admitting them, but giving in to something beyond your control, and I'm loath to do that.

I drive through the wide gates, with the Camp Cedar sign on my right, and turn the windshield wipers down. It's not even raining anymore, so I'm more self-conscious. I look as though I decided to take a shower with my clothes on. Stunning. I unbuckle my seat belt and sigh. The day is never complete unless Sierra and Sage have dumped on me, and considering how pathetic I look right now, they'll have plenty of ammunition.

I get out of the car and approach the main building at Camp Cedar. The organization has two parts: the coed day camp, where I went years ago, which is housed in an old *Sound of Music*–style lodge; and a gymnastics and dance program for older campers, where twelve-year-old Sierra and Sage perform ballet and do backbends that I could never do.

Kids holding various pieces of sporting equipment lounge around the benches outside, waiting for lifts home. This reminds me of how close I am to going back to high school—the countdown is at two weeks. Still, it feels as though any minute now the humidity-heavy trees will give way to the first signs of fall foliage, and I can't seem to quiet that slightly nervous voice inside telling me to make the most of what's left of my summer.

I scan the groups of campers but don't see my shiny, perky sisters. (They are tall for their age and tend to stick out, not like sore thumbs but like movie ingenues.) I have to go inside the building and bring this one-girl wet T-shirt contest to the masses. Silently, I thank the clothing gods who enabled me to choose dark shorts today rather than khakis that would showcase my red-and-white-polka-dot underwear (note: must remember to do laundry). Then, bracing myself for the worst, I walk through the front doors, past gawking boys and giggling girls who clearly notice that my arms are crossed over my chest for a reason. Or maybe I'm just paranoid.

"Nice boobs, Jenny!" Sierra yells from down the hall. She has Sage on her arm. Both of them are long-limbed and poised in their dance-floaty skirts and leotards, but they are not above laughing at me when I approach.

"Do you want a ride home or not?" I ask, dangling the car keys. It would be such great revenge to just turn around, walk away, and strand them in town. But then I'd probably feel guilty, not to mention risk getting in trouble. Ditching the twins isn't exactly "family bonding."

"You *have* to take us home," Sierra says.

"And you *have* to cover yourself!" Sage tacks her sentence on to Sierra's so it sounds like one fluid expression. They always seem to know what the other one is thinking and feeling. It kind of makes me jealous. I definitely don't have someone who is forever understanding me. "Mom'll ground you if you leave us here," she adds.

I would never really leave them to fend for themselves, especially not in their dance gear, but I squint at them to make it seem like it's a possibility. "Give me a shirt and I'll think about it."

Sage rummages through her backpack and produces a fine light blue shirt, but Sierra shakes her head. "Don't lend her that. It's your best one."

"Yeah, God forbid your *other* sister needs a favor." I sigh and reach for the tiny T-shirt, which will still be revealing, but at least not see-through.

"It's not that, Jenny," Sage protests. "It's just, like . . ." She doesn't even have to nudge Sierra to get her to complete the thought.

"You always get stuff on your clothes." Sierra looks at me and crumples her mouth.

"Am I really that bad?" I ask, laughing at myself. I let my hands drop to my sides, then notice that a couple of the guy counselors are checking out my rack and immediately cover myself again. I notice that my clothing is splattered with oil paint, stained from solvents, and generally in the wrinkled category. The twins are right. I am such a mess. "Forget it."

I hand Sage her T-shirt. It's only big enough for a preteen anyway. "Let's just go."

"Here," Sage says in an effort to make amends. "Take my backpack."

"I'm not your Sherpa." I flick her away.

"I was asking you to carry my bag so you could block your . . ." Sage gestures to my boobs.

"Oh." I'm so used to being left out of their twinliness that the few times a year they try to be nice, it slips right past me. "Well, I'm fine. I can handle the stares."

Sierra giggles and tosses her long, glossy golden hair over her shoulders. My wet hair is still plastered to my forehead. If I were produce, I would be rotting right now. Using my fingers like a comb, I try to sweep the hairs away. "What's so funny?" I ask Sierra, whose laughter has inspired Sage to giggle, too, in that annoyingly high-pitched preteen way that sends shivers down my arms.

Sierra laughs harder as we walk past the gym and the dance studios with their mirror-covered walls and ballet bars. "I have to ask. Did you do it on purpose?"

"Excuse me?" I stop and pivot so I'm facing them. Sierra and Sage tilt their heads and raise their eyebrows as though they are the cleverest almost-thirteen-year-olds in the world.

I'm so annoyed and bursting with frustration I could scream, but I don't. Instead, I say, "Yeah, that's right. I purposely hosed myself down with the sink sprayer at the art studio so I could humiliate myself when I came to pick you up from your stupid day camp."

Sage and Sierra are duly put in their places. However, as

10

they blush I realize they're blushing not only because I scolded them, but also because I have gained an audience of onlookers.

"I think you made your point," Sage says, gesturing to the campers, counselors, and parents who heard my brief speech.

"Let's go," I say, and walk out. I'm fuming, but not so much that I don't find relief when the crowd starts thinning out.

And I'm certainly not so lost in my annoyance that I miss him—a certain someone—lurking off to the side of the corridor. I try to pretend that he's not there in the same way I have tried to blink him away for the past two years. But it's a Herculean task, trying to forget how he smiles out of the side of his mouth, or not to notice how his brown hair has flecks of gold in it now. His skin is tan, too, most likely due to the hours and hours he spends outside, coaching peewee football. Blush creeps across my face. Maybe he didn't hear my tirade. Maybe he was doing whatever it is jocks do at the end of the day. High-five? Drink Gatorade? Stretch?

One of his friends snickers and points in my direction as we walk by them. "Hey, Tate. Did you check out that girl's—"

"Paint-splattered shorts? Yeah, they're kinda cool," Tate says just loudly enough, without making eye contact with me.

Tate's friend shrugs and says, "Whatever, dude," and wanders off.

I glance over at Tate for a millisecond, and he looks over

at me. Then he stares up at the ceiling thoughtfully, just like he used to do before he'd answer one of Mr. Connelly's questions in Am lit last year.

As I amble over to the car with the twins, I realize that, just like that, I've had my first, very indirect encounter with him. Tate Brodeur. The guy I like so much I can only say his name in my head. I wouldn't even admit to Faye, my best friend, how much I like him until she beat it out of me a few months ago during one of our Revolting Dessert evenings at her house, where we mixed instant pudding and cake mix, added whatever we found in the candy drawer, and baked it. Suffice it to say, Betty Crocker would not be pleased. But as we ate it I told her about my crush on Tate, and how it persists like a cough.

I want to tell Faye about this run-in right away. Only she's in the Berkshires in western Massachusetts doing some end-of-summer cooking program that sounds more like prison than cuisine class. While there, students are "not permitted any letters, calls, or e-mails" since that might "distract them from their goals." Is learning to make hollandaise sauce so mentally taxing you can't take a cell break for your best friend? But anyway, Faye's off-limits, so I can't tell her.

"Hello? Earth to booby." Sierra taps her fingernails on the car door to shake me back to reality. "Are you gonna let us in, or do we have to ride on the roof?"

"You suggested it," I say, and slide into the driver's seat. The twins sit in the back, already gossiping about their day, ignoring me and speaking their own language.

I turn up the radio, tune out their talk, and think about

what Sid said earlier. When will my paintings be better? I imagine a brilliant piece of art appearing in front of me. Then I imagine Tate in front of that art. I wish I'd said something to him, but I didn't. I wish I'd painted something amazing, but that didn't happen. And I wish I had someone to tell all this to.

But I don't.

TWO

"Think fast!" Russ shouts to me before I'm all the way out of the car or I realize there's a Frisbee headed toward my face. I have a quick choice to make: drop my painting supplies and catch the thing (which I might not even be able to do, given my lack of prowess in the hand-eye coordination department) or try to catch it while still holding all my crap (which seems doubly unlikely). So I duck, which causes the bright red Frisbee to sail past me and smack Sierra in the face.

"Ouch! What the . . . ," Sierra screams.

"Are you okay?" I ask.

"Why can't you just catch the thing like a normal person?" Sierra quips.

"Yeah. Could you *be* any less coordinated?" Sage says snidely. She squeezes Sierra's hand, showing more twin solidarity.

Russ trots over to us, shirtless and tan, all shoulders and smiles that make every girl in our neighborhood adore him.

"Hey, leave Jenny alone. It's not her fault. I snuck up on her."

I look at Russ and give him a silent *thank you* with my eyes. He raises his eyebrows as if to say *no problem*. Russ is the type of nice that is sometimes too nice. He always sees everyone's side, but isn't really able to stand by anyone in particular, as evidenced by his next comment.

"Sierra? You okay? Just be thankful you got the good genes. I know if I'd snuck a throw in on you guys, you'd both be able to catch it with your eyes closed."

And to think I was just about to ask Russ to come up to my room so he could see the mini sketches and paintings I've been working on in my room. Russ probably has no interest in that, though. I'm sure he'd rather not spend the last few hours of summer daylight inside when he could be running, chasing a ball, or doing anything where he can score a point or ten.

"Who's up for a game of volleyball?" Russ asks while twirling the Frisbee on his finger.

Sierra and Sage nod enthusiastically.

"Count me in, too!" Dad shouts from the study window upstairs that overlooks the driveway. He can hear offers for pickup basketball games, mentions of volleyball, or whispers of softball from miles away. He braces himself on the windowsill with his palms. "Hey, Jen. You'll spike for me, right?"

"No thanks, Dad," I say, shaking my head. The last time I played a nice Fitzgerald family game of volleyball, I sprained my wrist and couldn't paint for two weeks (except when I tried to use my other hand and my toes. I got the idea from this cool indie movie where the main character has to do that because of some accident and makes beautiful art that becomes internationally known. Let me just say that this is not what happened to me). "I'm going inside."

Dad looks at me a second longer, maybe waiting to see if I'll change my mind, but I shake my head again and slink into the house.

Inside, the house is cool and airy, scented with fruit.

"Smells good," I say as I start up the stairs. I'm on the third step when I see my mom in the kitchen, sitting on one of the breakfast stools by the counter. She's wearing a worn-in button-down rolled up to her elbows and a pair of running shorts. She turns around and bends a little in her seat so she can make eye contact with me.

"Want to taste?" Mom is already on her way to me with a wooden spoon before I can answer. When I *really* look at her, I see the twins—their slim frames, their grace and ease, their hair color (which reminds me of melting chocolate and butterscotch chips), their skin (which goes tan before summer has officially started), and their breezy way of walking (which is more like gliding). Even though I'm on the shorter side and have an average build, I always feel as though I'm clomping through life, splattering paint on clothing I just washed, managing to step in puddles I didn't even know were there.

I take a short inventory of my features as my mom reaches the staircase. Light eyes cloudy with rings of dark blue and a few flecks of yellow, and sometimes green. Hair that's usually kind of flat and stringy, but smooth to the touch when I get around to brushing it properly. Legs that are long and leanish, but not very toned or muscular, like the rest of my family's. It's only moments like this—just regular "would you like a taste" moments—that I am immediately hit with this sense of otherness.

Mom extends the wooden spoon, and I lean down for a quick sampling.

"Yum, it's good." I lick the marinade from my lips. "It stings, but in a good way. Is that chili powder?"

"Cayenne." Mom finishes what's left on the spoon herself. "We're all eating on the lawn tonight. Yard picnic."

I sigh. I wanted to paint. (And to daydream about Tate.) Picnicking will ultimately lead to games, which will lead to competition, which will lead to my being last picked for a team, or someone sighing because I'm on their team, or worse—being overly optimistic, like thinking *this* time I'll really pull through and whack/hit/kick catch the ball/disk/mallet/birdie.

"Mom?" I call out when she's back near the stove, flipping the chicken and drizzling the marinade on it in a haphazard fashion.

"Yes?"

"Did you . . ." I stop talking, but my feet take me into the kitchen for some reason. I'm wondering what exactly I wanted to say to her. I don't frequently confide in my mom about my crushes and painting critiques. But maybe I should try.

"Did something happen today?" Mom wipes her hand

on one of the towels (green-and-yellow pattern) she made to match the trim on the walls (green), which goes with the plates (yellow), and waltzes over to me.

"No, not really. I mean, Sid, the director at Downtown, he kind of said that—"

"Downtown. That's the studio, right?"

"Right." Sometimes I get the feeling that my mother has no idea what I'm really all about. "He's just so pompous. He was like . . ." I put on my Sid voice, all arrogant and faux Brit. "Your work is drivel and you'll thank me for saying so!"

I want my mom to console me. To laugh at Sid and hug me and say she knows he's full of crap and that she has every confidence that my work *is*—not *will be*—great. But what she says is, "Well, honey, maybe Sid has a point."

"What?" I can't hide the surprise in my voice. My mouth slacks.

Mom takes dinner dishes from the cabinet and begins to roll silverware into yellow-and-green-striped napkins. "Don't misunderstand me. You know Dad and I want you to do whatever makes you happy. But maybe . . ." She gestures at me with a fork. "Maybe painting isn't your *thing*."

"And maybe tennis or sled-driving or curling or skating *is*?" I can feel the annoyance bubbling inside my stomach. It burns more than the spices in the marinade. Of course it's at this moment my dad comes bounding down the stairs two at a time, having left his work up in his office, and overhears my sports mention.

"You're interested in tennis, Jenny? That's fantastic! When do you want to start?"

My mom goes back to preparing for the picnic, and I roll the rest of the silverware in napkins while I let my dad down yet again. "Actually, I was saying that painting—you know, brushes on canvas and so on—that's what I'm interested in. Still."

Dad squints at me. He's in his running gear: a faded Dartmouth T-shirt and yellow shorts that rustle when he walks. Soon it'll be cool enough for him to throw on the matching sweatshirt. I look at him and realize he matches the decor in here—green and yellow. Then I look at my own pale skin, streaked with cerulean and gold and red—lip red. In mid-October, when the leaves turn, I might match something then. But for now I'm at odds with the decor around here. And honestly, I'm used to it.

"I have to go get cleaned up, and then I'll help with dinner," I say.

Dad pats me on the back. Maybe he means it as genuine affection, but it registers as if I've somehow let the team down.

THREE

Water washes the day off my skin, sends the art criticism and wet T-shirt issue sliding to the floor. Little rivulets of paint run from my arms onto the white tiles in the shower stall, and I enjoy the peacefulness of being alone with my thoughts before I have to go sit on the family sidelines at dinner.

As I think, I find myself looking up, staring at nothing. I wonder why Tate Brodeur does this, and if he even knows he does it. He actually defended me when his friend was going to make a joke about me. A fairly heroic gesture for someone who runs in a different circle and whom I've only admired from a distance. I'd watch him in American lit last year, how he'd read aloud from the text and then glance up, thinking about the words. Or maybe he was just spacing out. He did the same thing at our school's spring fling last year. I remember eating a slice of pepperoni pizza near the refreshments table in the gym and watching him look up at nothing as he danced with pretty girl after pretty girl. I don't know. My guess is that he must see some sort of fire-works in his mind.

I want to experience those explosions of color firsthand someday and know precisely what he's thinking, but we would actually have to speak for this to happen. And we haven't, because he is, of all things, a jock. Maybe we're not at opposite ends of the social spectrum, but we're not a natural overlap.

Still, he seems to be so much more than the category he naturally falls into. He's always spouting obscure sports trivia to other jocky guys (example: What was the Mills Commission?) who never have the correct answer, so I know he's smart, too. I want to tell him that I want to know him, or that I like the way I smile after he walks by. I want to tell him that the Mills Commission was appointed in 1905 to determine the origin of baseball (just because I eschew all activities sporty doesn't mean the jumble of family talks hasn't seeped in; I know more stats and facts than I'll ever need). I want to show him how I paint fireworks on the canvas, all lights and colors spreading out into darkness.

It's funny how you can't exactly pick your crush. Well, you can, but once it gets hold of you it's hard to shake off. I mean, Tate Brodeur isn't whom I thought I'd like. Normally, I'm drawn to the brooding, slouching drama boys or their visual arts counterparts, all hip and retro with glasses or with accents from faraway places. But Tate's about as commercial as you can get without being boring. I like his tilted mouth, the way he always appears to be looking closely at life, seeing the details like I do. Plus, he's beautiful. Good-looking like the lead in a Disney dogsledding movie—all outdoorsy, but sensitive in his well-worn T-shirts and faded jeans.

I wrap myself in an oversized white towel and use the back of my hand to swipe the mirror clean. Outside, Russ, Sierra, and Sage are engaged in some sort of tag game that involves throwing whole lemons at each other. My mother is half-playing; my father is grilling the chicken. I can see them all, the five of them, from the bathroom window. They look happy. Complete. Matching. I imagine the same scene except with me in it and feel lonely all over again, imagining myself on the picnic blanket while they pound each other with citrus fruits.

I take a minute to study my face in the mirror. I'm maybe a shade darker than my winter self, meaning not entirely translucent. A knock at the door is followed by my mother's face peeking through a slim crack.

"There you are." Mom's hand clutches the doorknob. "Good shower?"

"Yep, now I've moved on to questioning my existence." I smile at her while I shake my hair out of its twist.

Mom smirks. "Oh, a little light pondering for the day?"

She gets me half of the time, and the other half it's as if the only thing she recognizes is my exterior—the light brown swash of freckles over my nose and cheeks, the way my mouth has a full lower lip and two sharp points on top, how my hair is just a shade too light to be true brown and a few shades too dark to be interesting. "I didn't mean to insult you before, Jenny. I only meant to say that sometimes when you have to struggle really hard with things—"

"I know; try, try again."

Mom shakes her head. "No. I was going to say that every once in a while if you struggle and struggle and nothing happens, then maybe it's time to move on."

"So are you saying that Sid was right? That I have no artistic talent?" I watch my mother, wait for her to dispute what I've said. She doesn't. "He said I'd get better." Did he? Or did he only mean that I suck now and might not suck as much in the future?

"Okay," Mom says, and starts to close the door. "But think about tennis. It could be fun. You and Russ could take on the twins." She pauses to see if I'll take the family-bonding bait. No chance. "Food's almost ready."

It's not that I lack the guts to stand up for myself, because I could. I could stand here, hands on my hips in arguing mode, and try to convince her that painting is my passion, that I will succeed. But I acknowledge that perhaps I'd be suffering from the Shakespearean "The lady doth protest too much" syndrome—if I have to be so vehement about my feelings, maybe I'm just in denial about what's real. Maybe one of the reasons I don't express myself as well as I want to is because inside, shoved way down into an unseen pit, I'm not sure of what I want.

Left in the steam with my own reflection, I allow myself to wonder about what I wouldn't vocalize to my parents back in the kitchen. The twins look like Mom, and Russet is my dad's mini self. Maybe I have a little of my mother's cheeks, and the freckles could be hers. But the artistic side? My hair that's unlike anyone's? The ring of green in my otherwise blue eyes?

They could be from him.

Mom and Dad were open from the beginning. They figured letting me (as well as Sage, Sierra, and Russ) all know about him would be better than our stumbling onto the fact of him later in life.

The fact being that my biological dad is Donor 142.

Mom had me back when she was super work-focused and single and thought she'd be alone forever. Of course, she got pregnant (after choosing 142 from the other donors), met my actual dad, and had me. They got married when I was one, and he legally adopted me and raised me, and here we all are. The Fitzgeralds. Russ shrugged when the early incarnation of Team Fitzgerald (me, Mom, Dad) told him. He was four at the time, and I don't even know if it made sense to him. "Who cares?" he said while he bounced a rubber ball off the wall in his room. "We're all the same."

All the same. It's pretty much what anyone says when they find out, although it's not something I advertise. Regardless, no one in my family really seems to make the connection between this fact and how I'm different from them. But I do. I can't help it.

I wonder about my genes and if they direct me toward paints and palettes rather than field kicks and playing center forward. Somehow, imagining who could be out there, where I could have come from, and how my DNA will play itself out makes me feel less alone. I love my family, of course I do. Only, I'm not totally connected to them. Like that circle I was painting today, kind of off to the side, almost falling off the canvas. When I think of where I came from, I imagine strings connecting me to someone else. And maybe it's that wondering that will pull the sliding circle from the side of the canvas to the center.

"Jenny!" Russ shouts from downstairs.

I open the bathroom door and step into the hallway, the steam wafting behind me. "Just a second!" I hang up my damp towel, slide into flip-flops, a white tank top, and old jeans (the ones that fit so well I refuse to chuck them even though they are threadbare in places and hang a little low). They remind me of summer and beaches and feel cozy. Two weeks until school starts. Two weeks until the art show at Downtown Studios. Two weeks for me to cough up something real on the canvas and real in my life so this summer is memorable.

I look out the upstairs window to where my dad is juggling lemons while my mom runs sprint races from the patio to the edge of the unfinished area of our backyard with Sierra and Sage. They stop at the line of dirt and pile of gravel near the wooded area, then race back to the limestone patio and wooden deck. Dad is always meaning to finish the landscaping job, but with work and summer sports, I guess he hasn't found the time. I half-expect to find Russ talking to Faye, my best friend, while he kicks at some loose gravel by the barbecue, but then I remember Faye's still away at her gourmet chef classes. Cupping my hand to the glass, I peer closer to see who he's talking to. A shiver creeps over my bare arms and jean-covered legs when I see that it's Tate Brodeur, and he's looking up, as usual.

Only this time it's at me.

FOUR

I can paint in my mind reasons why Tate Brodeur would grace my backyard with his presence:

(1) He's lost.

(2) He has an urgent message from Camp Cedar for Sierra and Sage.

(3) Now that summer is ending, he's looking for yard work to make extra money and sees the gravel pile and dirt-encrusted rocks at the back of our yard as his chance to score big.

Of course none of the reasons listed is the one I'm hoping is true. I make my way down the staircase, my hair wet on my neck, my pulse racing, to the backyard. From the sliding glass door at the far end of the kitchen I watch how relaxed Tate looks with Russ. They're tossing a Nerf football back and forth as they talk. Sierra and Sage sneak a few glances at Tate and giggle.

"Jenny!" My mom's voice is muffled behind the sliding door until I open it and her true volume registers. *"Jennnn-y!"*

"I'm right here." My flip-flops make funny noises as I

walk onto the patio. It's one of those entrances that make me cringe: too much attention on my arrival. I prefer to slip into a scene without much fanfare.

"So glad you can join us!" my dad booms, gesturing at me with the tongs he uses to flip steaks or barbecued chicken, or whatever it is we're having tonight.

"I like your shirt," Sierra says, and points to my tank top.

"Dry looks good on you." Sage laughs.

Nice. Why is it that their snide remarks make me so annoyed? On a normal evening I might spit out a nasty retort that my parents would send me back to my room for (and without dinner, I might add). But this is not a normal evening. Tate Brodeur is a few feet away, catching passes from Russ and looking over at me.

Maybe the reason he's here in my backyard, decked out in his beach-worn green shorts and trashed sneakers, is the reason I didn't have the heart to add to the list before: maybe Tate is here to see me.

"Hey, Fitz," Tate says.

"Hey," I say to him, but Russ jogs over and elbows me.

"He means me, Jenny." Russ's forehead glows with sweat, and he knocks the football from Tate's hands. "You two know each other?"

I look at Tate directly for probably the first time ever, and he stares back. A grin spreads over his face, and I return the expression. Life is good. Tate steps forward and offers his hand. "I don't think we've ever been formally introduced," he says.

Ever the host, Russ pulls me by the hand so I can shake Tate's. "Tate Brodeur, Jenny Fitzgerald. There ya go."

If only Russ knew that the introduction was hardly necessary. For two years all I've done is fantasize about this moment.

"Hey." I feel my pulse speed up as our hands are about to make contact. He grips my hand, but he doesn't turn his gaze away from me for a full five seconds. Maybe it's less. I can't count when I'm near him, because most of my brainpower is spent trying to resist him.

And why must I resist him? There are several reasons. First, he's not my type—i.e., he doesn't wear ripped T-shirts and flaunt a knowledge of art house films, etc. Second, most people call him Bro, which is just ridiculous, and I have no idea why he allows this. Third, Tate and I could never survive as a couple at our high school, because I circulate on the periphery of the cliques. I'm what you would call a floater—not preppy enough to be a cheerleader, not bookish enough to be a wonk, not sporty enough to be a jock (not sporty in the slightest), and not bland enough to be anonymous. This last reason makes liking him pretty damn near futile.

Still, I want to know Tate's reason for being here more than anything. And then it's clear.

"I came by to inform your brother that he's got a good chance of making varsity this year."

"Oh yeah?" Reality has a nasty way of making me feel like an idiot for dreaming. "Well, Russ is a football superstar, that's for sure." I pat my brother on the back. He's impossible not to like with his easygoing manner and was born to be a professional athlete, unlike me.

"Varsity would rock big-time." Russ chucks the football up into the air, where mosquitoes swirl. Russ looks at me. "Then you could come and watch!"

Russ's excitement about the possibility of becoming one of the youngest players, if not *the* youngest player ever on our high school varsity team makes me sad for a brief moment. He seems so much closer to achieving what he wants than I am, so much closer to being the person he was meant to be. Plus, lucky him, he'll be near Tate, the star quarterback.

"A couple minutes and we'll be all set for dinner." My mom wipes her hands on a green-and-yellow dish towel, playfully swatting me on her way to the kitchen. "Russ, is your friend going to stay?"

Mom's words seem so sharp just then. Tate is my brother's friend, and not connected to me in the least. Isn't that priceless?

"What about it, Bro?" Russ asks Tate.

Tate shrugs with one shoulder and then quickly looks up at the sky à la his thinking mode. I notice how his eyebrows are raised, and it immediately makes him a zillion times cuter. "I actually have to get going. I'm in charge of trivia night at camp." He sighs and then puts on a game show host voice. "Welcome to Camp Cedar's annual Sports Quiz." Then he stops. "That's about as far as I've gotten."

"Dude, that's lame," Russ laughs. From the grill, a puff of smoke sends my mom running over from the kitchen with her dish towel flailing. Always affable, Russ goes over to see how he can help, while Sierra and Sage do simultaneous cartwheels across the lawn, leaving me alone with Tate. Then I realize that one part of me is able to do a backflip— my heart.

"So, are you a master of sports trivia?" I twist my still-damp hair up off my neck so it stays in a loose bun.

Tate palms the Nerf ball, then holds it between both hands, and for once I wish I were good at sports. "Not a master per se. More like a blue belt."

"Not bad." I cross my arms as a line of defense, as if he could see right inside to where my crush is hiding.

Tate throws a mini spiral and catches the ball. "What about you?" He puts on the game show host voice again. "Can you tell me what the sport is with the fastest moving object?"

"Jai alai," I say automatically. Tate looks shocked, his mouth agape. "I've been schooled for sixteen years at the Fitzgerald Academy." I tap the side of my head with my finger as if to indicate my brain is filled with a lot more useless information.

"Impressive." Tate kicks his sneakers into the grass, making them squeak. I can see my mom plating food while Russ takes over the grill so my dad can chase the twins with the garden hose. They squeal and laugh, falling on each other on the thick dark grass.

"Yeah, well, you never know when that stuff will come in handy." And it already has.

I always know when I'm happy, because my eyes start to play tricks on me, letting whatever it is that's bringing me joy start to looked painted. Tate's mouth becomes a swirl of dark red; in his hair I see brushstrokes of bark-colored brown, a few streaks of summer copper. It's like a van Gogh, all eddies of color. Suddenly I want nothing more than to be in my room, translating the picture in my head onto canvas.

"Here." Tate suddenly throws the ball my way, breaking the painty happiness collage.

"Huh?" I try to grasp the squish of it. Even with my lack of coordination, the catch should be possible, but I'm caught off guard, so it thwacks against my stomach and lands on the ground.

"Sorry." Tate squats to pick up the ball and then points to my ankle. "Interesting tattoo."

I check out the dollop of orange smeared on my skin. Now I have something else to be embarrassed about. "Oh, it's just oil paint. It didn't come off in the shower." All of a sudden my urge to retreat becomes too much for me to handle. "I should go eat dinner," I say, gesturing to the picnic table, where Russ is scooping a mound of potato salad onto his plate.

"Oh." Tate looks at the rest of my family and then back at me. He pauses, his lips partway open so it looks like he's about to say something important. Then he shakes his head. "Well, I guess I'll see you around?"

I nod, even though we probably won't see each other around. I'm not likely to be one of those girls who watches preseason practice, pointing to the hot quarterback and bringing the team ice water. Tate's not likely to show up randomly at Downtown Studios. "Sure."

"Hey, Fitz! See you later!" Tate yells to my brother, who is too busy snarfing food to do anything other than give a lax wave. Tate nods at me and then saunters off to his beat-up Hershey-bar-colored Volvo in the driveway.

"Jenny, come and get it!" My mom flags me over to the table. When she notices I'm not taking strides toward the group, she cups her hands megaphone-style and adds, "Now, Jenny!"

Tate's a few yards away when he stops, turns back to me, and asks, "So, how fast is fast, anyway?"

Without having to ask for clarification, I know what he means. "The jai alai pelota's been clocked at one hundred eighty-eight miles per hour."

"Amazing. Even I didn't know that," he yells back, and I get chills.

"There's more where that came from," I shout, and take a step toward my parents. I can tell they're annoyed that I'm delaying the family dinner, because my mother has her hands on her hips, waiting to start her food until I'm there.

"I bet," Tate says, his car keys swinging from his fingers. "I'll be at Callahan's later if you feel like intimidating everyone with your superior knowledge."

Callahan's is the local hangout at the mall. Everyone goes there to talk the night away trying to figure out where else to go. It's not a place I frequent. In fact, it's not a place I've been to much at all. Faye and I usually spend time at the Shoreline Diner instead, where ancient waitresses serve coffee and doughnuts and there's no crowd of jocks trying to make a basket by chucking napkins into the trash cans.

Tate gives one quick wave and shuts the car door. He drives off, leaving a spray of gravel from the back tires and me with my mind racing. Did he tell me that he'd be at

Callahan's so I should go there to meet him? Or was it more like, if I happened to be there, and he happened to also, we could hang out?

"Jenny! We're waiting." Dad stands up from the table and speaks in his business phone call voice, which means I better listen.

So I do.

FIVE

The night air moves in, and with the rolling dark, the automatic patio lights flick on. I manage to eat dinner, pass the ketchup, nod at Sierra's gymnastics story, ask my mother about her day, and listen as my father talks about his job as a divorce mediator.

"It's just so much more civil, don't you think?" Dad asks. "They never even raised their voices."

"Definitely." Russ nods and chews.

"Without a doubt," my mother adds. Then, to all of us, she keeps going. "You're lucky to have parents who have admirable jobs. Dad could be one of those cutthroat divorce lawyers with no scruples. But instead, he took the higher ground and really helps people achieve their goals without cruelty."

My mom worked in Hollywood as a script doctor before meeting my dad, and sometimes she gives mini speeches that sound like she's still employed by a film company. She worked crazy hours and had (in her words) absolutely no social life that didn't revolve around the office, which is what led to her "decision." No one in my family considers this subject a big enough deal to talk much about, though, including me. Even if I think about it sometimes, I don't vocalize it. Maybe there's a difference between being honest about the details of my conception, which my parents have been with me from the start, and being open to the possibility that there are larger ramifications at work here, which maybe hasn't been the case.

Big info is like that, though. You try to convince yourself that it's just the knowing or not knowing that matters. But really it's more than just finding out you're adopted or from a donor or whatever. You have to build that into your life. And that's what my parents don't want to do; they'd rather say it once, then tuck it back into hiding.

Family is family, and I love mine. However, I always seem to carry this sense of otherness with me. I feel a difference even though there's not supposed to be one. It's nothing solid, nothing tangible I can point to. I can't compare this to what it's like when someone is adopted. All I know is with this, it's like being half in and half out.

"Aren't we proud of Dad and his mediation skills? His ability to aid people in their struggles to connect?" My mom beams at my dad. She left Hollywood with my dad, and they settled back east. Now my mom writes pamphlets for businesses, talking up hardware stores or local graphic design firms, trying to make each store or person as compelling as the latest blockbuster movie.

"That's great, Dad," I say, just so they know I'm paying attention.

The twins pick at each other's plates, each one knowing

that the other likes hummus but not mustard on her chicken, allowing each other to sample the dill pickles or chips without complaining. I reach for one of Sage's sour cream and onion chips. She swats me away with a slap on the hand.

"Back off," she says, and snatches the chip for herself.

"Give me a break." I shake my head.

"You could share, Sierra," my mother says, and then corrects herself. "I mean, Sage."

They don't mind being confused. It's as though they exist on Earth as one combined force.

"Never mind," I say, and wipe my mouth on a napkin. "I'm heading in."

"To the Batcave," Russ says. He means it as a joke, but it's all my dad needs to start in on me.

"Just like that?" Dad gestures at me with a baby carrot but doesn't say anything else.

"I had dinner," I say as though that's justification. I untwist my hair so it falls down on my shoulders, catching the last of the sunlight and warming my neck.

"I thought we could move the sand from the garage tonight," Dad says, referring to the backyard landscaping mission.

I stand up. "I can't tonight, Dad."

"C'mon, Jenny," my father urges.

Mom starts stacking the plates, and I help her gather cutlery, sticking forks, spoons, and knives into an empty cup so they stick up like a flower arrangement.

"Sorry. My artwork calls."

"Have fun in your closet," Russ says in his good-natured voice.

Last year I turned my closet into the smallest studio ever. There's no light, hardly any room, and no way in hell it could ever really be deemed a studio, but it gives me a little bit of room to call my own. The shelves are stocked with canvas, wooden frames, and containers I recycled that once held my parents' gourmet sauces and are now filled with paint.

"We want to go to the mall." Sierra's and Sage's voices overlap. "Please? Missy Walters invited us." Sage elbows Sierra.

Missy Walters is a girl in their class who skipped over princess-in-training and went straight to queen bee. I fight the urge to roll my eyes at the twins and their wannabe-cool outings, but I do know what it's like to want to be included.

"Richard, can you take them?" my mother asks my father.

"I'm done driving. I went to Ridgefield and back today already for a client proposal," Dad says, passing the buck.

I can feel it coming. I know Mom is going to ask me, so I try and beat her to the punch. "I can't drive them, either. There's an art show. At Downtown Studios. And it's the biggest—"

I flounder for words, which just proves how important the show is to me. At the same time, I highly doubt my parents are going to squeal with delight over my news. Although, if there were a contest or competition involved, their ears might perk up.

I swallow hard and continue. "It's in about two weeks, after the county carnival, and the director said if he likes my work, he'll put it in the exhibit." I watch my mother as she flaps open a garbage bag, shoving the lemonade-sticky cups and empty bag of chips inside. Is she even listening? "Anyway, it's a pretty big deal, so I have to work extremely hard."

"Sounds cool," Russ says, staring at me blankly. I see my parents give each other *the look,* the look that my mom gave me today when she hinted that maybe painting isn't *my thing.* All I want is for my dad to slam his hand on the table and demand I go paint, the way he does on the few occasions Russ slacks off on his training.

Sierra ignores me and taps my dad on the shoulder. "Daddy, please? Missy's never invited us to the mall before." Dad doesn't respond. I notice Sage nudge Sierra in the ribs, another twin moment.

Sierra clicks into action. "Besides, if we go to the mall tonight, we could get our cleats for fall soccer."

I know exactly what Sierra is doing and that it's going to work like all her plans do. Still, my mind is obsessing over the fact that I only have fourteen days to produce some art that's worthy of being shown.

My dad puts his hand on Sierra's shoulder. "If you don't have adequate gear, you better get it soon. Nothing worse than stiff new shoes at a real game." Russ nods as though my father has passed on some sage advice.

My mom touches my arm. Here we go. "Jenny, I know you have some work you'd like to do, but—"

Dad steps in so that he can complete the parental unit powerhouse. "Be a team player, Jen." He makes a sweeping motion encompassing all of us clustered around the table.

The light is fading, and so is my hope of painting tonight. "Give them a ride, will you?"

My sisters nod and look earnest, but their eyes suggest a smugness I can't call them on right now. He doesn't say it, but I can see in his eyes the phrase *Your "hobby" can wait.*

I breathe in to steady my nerves. I don't want to pitch a fit about this, because in the end I'll end up feeling guilty about it. Then all of a sudden goose bumps prickle up my arms as I think about who else might be at the mall.

Maybe my hobby can wait for just a little while.

SIX

My chocolate-and-barely-pink sweatshirt is zipped up to my neck, but it doesn't quite protect my pounding heart. I am no sooner through the Cutler Green Mall's front doors with Sierra and Sage than they race off together, leaving me alone to wander through the throngs of summertime shoppers and fend for myself.

"Be back here at ten," I yell after them, and they do me the small favor of acknowledging me with a wave. This is the last couple weeks of the mall's extended hours—even retail counts down to fall. A couple weeks from now, the storefronts will darken at six and the twins will be forced to face homework, not shopping. And so will I.

With my sketchbook in hand, I head toward Callahan's. I could wander around, check out the scene there, and play it cool, but the truth is, playing it cool doesn't come that easily to me. Instead of braving the crowd inside Callahan's, I sit down on a bench between the Gap and Wilsons Leather. *It has a nice view of the fountain,* I think. But I'm not convinced—I am being a coward.

I spend the next few minutes people-watching and recognize a lot of the kids here. They are splintered into the usual groups that form in the school cafeteria. The disgruntled rockers are making the rounds at Hot Topic. The bronzed, ponytailed girls have shopping bags swinging from each hand, unplagued by the bills they're sticking their parents with. The sports crew huddles outside Strauss Sporting Goods, close enough to me that I can put a name to all the faces. I take note that someone is missing from their group.

I flip open my sketchbook to my latest design—two circles that meet midway on the page. It's like the painting I was working on today, the one Sid deemed first-grade material. Unfortunately, now that I'm staring at it, I can see Sid's point. Something's not right here. Even though this design looks deep and meaningful in my mind, when I put it on the canvas it seems juvenile and amateurish. Regardless, I take two pencils—one red, one blue—from my bag and attempt to fix it somehow. Moving the red pencil at an angle, I shade a half-moon shape and then use the blue pencil to highlight it. Hmmm. Not bad.

"How's it going, Degas?" The voice is coming from above me. I look up and see Tate staring intently at my sketchbook. Instinctually, I slam the thing shut. It doubles as a kind of journal, with random thoughts and titles of paintings scribbled here and there. I never want anyone to look at it. "Sorry. Am I interrupting?" he asks.

I blink a few times and regain my composure. Degas painted dancers mainly, but I don't think about that. Instead, I think about the fact that Tate's actually talking to me. "No. Not at all."

41

Tate grins at me and raises an eyebrow. "Really?" He bends down and puts a finger on my book. "Are you sure?"

It's as if he wants me to be real with him, so I say, "Okay, maybe a little. But I don't mind."

"Cool." Tate waves to his pack of guys but doesn't join them as they wander into Callahan's, where they will most likely hunch over plates of fries and gallons of soda. He brushes a hand through his hair and sits down next to me. "So, tell me something I don't know about sports. Test me."

"Okay." My lungs fill with air as I think of what to say. Again the painted images of Tate start to appear. What colors would I use to capture the greens, blues, and gold in his eyes? "I can't think of anything."

"That's okay." He pauses. "I like to talk about other things, too, you know."

I tilt my head to the right in disbelief. "Yeah? Like what?"

He drums his fingers on the edge of the bench. "Geography, for one. When I was a kid, I read the atlas like it was a comic book." His smile is flawless. "Don't slap the loser label on my forehead just yet. I also know a lot about art—paintings and sculptures and stuff."

Of course this gets my attention, but then I wonder if he's doing that guy thing. Faye says boys will find out what you like, drop a few names about it—for instance, calling you by the name of a famous artist you admire—and then assume you'll let them into your pants. So I ignore the art comment from Tate and go back to sports. I'd rather stay on his turf. Talking about art would be way too personal for me, and even though I want to get close to him, I'm not ready for it yet.

"I'll stick with sports trivia, thanks. But it's nice to know you're so well-rounded." I blush at the thought of how flirty that just sounded.

"You think you're up to the challenge?" Tate leans toward me a little as though he's about to take one of my hands in his. He doesn't, of course, but the thought of it makes me so nervous I bite my lip to keep from freaking out.

"I can handle it," I say.

Tate puts on his game show host voice again. "In the four major U.S. pro sports—wait, you do know what those are, right?"

I sigh heavily and roll my eyes. "Baseball, football, basketball, and hockey."

Tate twists his mouth in agreement. "Just checking." He pauses and looks up, probably trying to remember what he was going to ask. Meanwhile, more of his cronies walk by and stare, no doubt wondering what their studly leader is doing with a girl best known at school for the new mural on the wall outside the guidance office. "There are only a few teams whose names do not end with an s. Name them."

I narrow my eyes. "You couldn't come up with anything better? Come on. Basketball: the Miami Heat, the Utah Jazz, the Orlando Magic. Baseball: the Boston Red Sox, the Chicago White Sox. Hockey: the Colorado Avalanche, the Minnesota Wild, the Tampa Bay Lightning . . ."

"And football?" Tate asks, his smirk indicating that he's impressed. Who knew the hours I spent sucking up info from Russ, the twins, and my parents might one day come in handy?

"Football? None." I cross my arms over my chest. "Satisfied?"

Tate shrugs. "Now it's my turn to be quizzed." He stands up and motions for me to do the same, leading me to the nearest escalator.

I follow him, wondering where he'll take me and what on earth he could possibly show me. When we're outside the giant bookstore, he points inside. "Quiz me."

Weaving through aisles of novels, past the bestsellers and the small café at the back, right next to the magazine racks we get to what, in my opinion, is the best area of the store—oversized art books, their thick pages spread with images of paintings and drawings, hulk the shelves. "Are you sure we're in the right section?"

Tate grabs a book of artwork from the Museum of Modern Art and hands it to me, our fingers close enough that they touch just for a millisecond. "Go."

I flip the book open and display a painting of swirls and the night sky, but I keep the title of the work and its artist hidden with my hand. "What's this?"

"*The Starry Night* by van Gogh," Tate says flatly. "Too easy. Try again."

I page through the book and test him some more. Each time he responds correctly: Seurat, Gauguin, Mondrian. Finally, I catch him. "And this one?"

Tate scratches his neck as he wonders. Knowing that I am the reason for his remembering stance makes me feel special. "Matisse? No. Wait. Miró."

I shake my head. "František Kupka. It's called *The First Step*." I wonder if that could be the title of our evening, too. "See the shapes?" I point to the painting. "I love how he takes this thing that's so familiar, just a regular old circle, and makes it, I don't know, magical."

Tate nods and touches the page where the big center circle seems to split itself in two, the shapes overlapping. "Luminescent. It's like they're connected, but they're not."

"Exactly," I say. Then my pulse steadies, instead of racing as I would have expected. Calm washes over me. Tate obviously understands the painting, and I can't help but feel that he understands me, too. I gaze at the circles again and it hits me. "Oh my God, that's just what I'm trying to say."

"What do you mean?"

I take out my sketchbook and flip it open to the red-and-blue drawing. "Here, like this." I'm so excited to have figured this out that I don't hesitate to show my book to him. Tate leans in close, his eyes on the page, truly interested. "See?" I say. "The circles are doubled, like twins, but not quite."

"Wow, you're right," he replies.

A small silence grows between us, and suddenly we're a little weirded out by it. Tate coughs and takes a few steps back until he's safe in the next section over. The magazine aisles are jammed with covers that feature glossy photos of starlets, makeover tips, and country houses. One cover asks, "Do You Like Him? Take Our Quiz and Find Out." But I've already taken a quiz tonight and know the resounding answer.

I close the art book and put it back on the shelf. Then I walk over to where he's standing and grab a random magazine off the rack. I read aloud in a mocking voice. "Top ten ways to get *him* to notice *you*. One: dress for success." Tate cracks up and strikes a JCPenney catalog pose.

"What? Don't I belong on the cover of *Esquire* or something?" Tate asks, making me laugh.

"Number three is 'Tell him something no one else knows. He'll feel superspecial.' "

Tate laughs. "Oh, I don't know if I'm up for that." He grabs another magazine off the rack and reads to me from some dry article about mortgage rates and insurance premiums until I do a giant fake yawn. "Okay, I'm losing my audience. Hold on." Tate tosses the finance mag on a nearby chair and snags a glossy *Teen Vogue*. "Are your friends stealing your style?"

I pluck at my zipped-up sweatshirt. "Who would want to? Next question."

"Could donor number forty-nine be your father?" Tate asks in an over-the-top manner.

Once I realize what he's talking about, my face falls a little. I wasn't expecting this information to come out this way, or so soon. Tate looks up at me, unaware of what my sullen expression means. So I explain. "Actually, my donor father is number one-forty-two."

The magazine droops in Tate's hands. He seems a little embarrassed. "Really?"

I nod. "It's no big deal, though."

Tate keeps hold of the magazine but sits on the floor. He pats the carpet next to him, so I sit there, slouching amid the home renovation guides and soap opera mags. "It seems like a big deal."

I shrug. "I grew up knowing this, so it's just a part of my life. I don't know. Sometimes I think it's kind of like having a scar, but without any memory of the injury. Does that make sense?"

Tate grins. "It does."

I take a deep breath and exhale. Talking with him is so much easier than I'd ever imagined, like the best kind of painting, where the images seep out from my mind onto the canvas without any hesitation.

"So how does this work? Is Russ your real brother?"

"Well. It's like this: Russ, Sierra, and Sage are all fully related biologically to each other. But only half to me." As I say this out loud—out of the context of my head and off the pages of my sketchbook, too—the sentence sounds weird. Especially the word *half*.

"And what's your story?"

Tate and I lock eyes, and for a split second I think he's going to lean forward and kiss me right here in the chain bookstore. But he doesn't. He just waits for me to talk. "Well, seventeen years ago, after a lunch meeting in Santa Monica, my mom visited a doctor's office off of Montana Avenue and picked a donor, and a few weeks later got inseminated with donor sperm, and voilà! I made it into the world nine months later."

"Sounds like you've got that story down pat," Tate says.

"Meaning?" I ask.

"Meaning it sounds kind of rehearsed." Tate sighs. "I guess I'm interested in what you actually *think* about it."

He's right. It does sound rehearsed. My parents told me this info just once in my lifetime, and somewhere along the line I'd detached myself from what it all meant, even though in the back of my mind it was always a part of my thoughts. Now Tate wants to hear my thoughts, but I can't find it within myself to dig that deep. "I don't know."

Tate looks confused. "Huh."

"What?"

"Never mind. I don't want to pressure you to spill your guts at a Barnes and Noble superstore."

I smile widely. He doesn't want to pressure me. How sweet is that?

I glance down at my shoes and try to formulate what I do think, and how I'm going to express that to Tate. I can feel Tate watching me, and then I hear him turning the pages of a magazine.

Without warning, a bunch of words come bubbling out of my mouth.

"Even though I love my family, I guess there's a part of me that . . . I don't know how to describe it. Maybe it'd be easier to draw what I mean." I pause and look up at Tate. Tate has his eyes glued to the magazine. My heart sinks because he's not paying attention.

Still, I keep talking. "Maybe there's this part of me that wonders what's out there in the future—"

"You mean who. *Who* is out there?" he says emphatically, his eyes widening as he continues to read. Then he looks at me excitedly, as though he's stumbled onto a treasure map or something. "Jenny, this article is all about these kids like you. They have donor dads and—"

"No," I interrupt. "I'm not desperate to find the donor. I have my dad." For some reason a memory of my father pops into my brain. When I was little, he let me draw on the wall in his office. He'd also mark my height with a crayon and write the date. He's long since painted over the wall art, but I wonder what he thinks of that growth chart now, and whether he remembers each inch I grew and when I stopped marking time in there with him.

"Wait, listen to me for a sec." Tate puts his hand over my mouth playfully to silence me. I can feel his palm on my chin and cheek. His skin is calloused from a summer of throwing passes, but I couldn't care less. He feels amazing. "This isn't about finding the donor."

Part of me wants to see where Tate is going with this, and part of me feels uncomfortable with these questions. I glance at my watch in an attempt to stall and notice how late it is. "Crap, I have to meet the twins," I say, and stand up. I can't believe how fast the time has gone.

"The twins can wait," Tate says, standing up so he can look me in the face. "Read this. I'm going to buy a copy."

He shows me the magazine article. He's close enough that I can feel his breath on my cheek, and I am torn between wanting to enjoy this fraction of time with him and wanting to go. If I found it hard to have a crush on him before, after tonight I'm doomed to lust after him forever. "Fine, I'll read it."

"Be back in a second." He walks off toward the cash

49

registers with another copy of the magazine rolled up in his hand.

Alone with only the stacks of periodicals for company, I consider just shelving the magazine. I really don't need the extra brain clutter of wondering about a guy I'll never meet, even if he is the one who helped bring me into this world. I have enough on my mind. I have to leave Tate behind in less than ten minutes. What if I never see him again? Or, more likely, what if I see him again, but it's like tonight never happened?

Tate doesn't look at me from where he stands in line. He just flips through the pages of *Teen Vogue,* not caring who sees him with it. Then, when I think he's forgotten about me, he looks up, smiles, and points to the article, mouthing the words *I said read.*

I smile back and obey, unaware that in a few days this one moment will have changed everything.

SEVEN

Nothing prepares you for change. All of a sudden the unexpected can drop into your lap and wake you up from your napping life. On the drive back from the mall, this is how I feel: awake. Eyes wide, I watch the road, aware of Sierra and Sage in the backseat, chattering away about cleats and boys and cool clothes. But I'm so wrapped up in my thoughts that I don't say a word to them. They have each other, and don't need me invading their world.

My world is brewing with possibilities. I think back to how Tate paid for the magazine and handed it to me as I finished skim-reading the article.

"So, what do you think?" he asked as we walked back into the mall's atrium, the arched walkways dotted with large ferns and plants so green and shiny they looked fake.

"I think . . . I'm confused" was all I could get out.

"Will you look into it?" Tate pointed to the cover of the magazine, where the title of the article was written in a bold orange font. "And maybe call me when you decide what to do?"

"Maybe," I said, sounding far calmer than I felt. I had waited for so long for Tate to give me his phone number, but I never thought it would be under these circumstances. I wanted to be excited, but I was so anxious, the happiness of this monumental achievement was almost lost to me.

"Do you have your cell with you? I can just add myself to your contacts list."

Cell phone? I spilled paint thinner on it a couple of weeks ago, which rendered it completely useless. Dad refused to buy me a new one, but Mom has been arguing in my defense, probably because she wants to be able to contact me whenever the twins need their butts kissed.

"No, it's kind of MIA," I said.

He jotted his number down on a slip of paper and gave it to me.

Now I'm thinking about how I closely watched his hands and noticed that he's a lefty. I read somewhere that the right hemisphere of the brain is more active in left-handed people, and therefore they are more visual and have more artistic skill. I can't wait to find out on my own if this theory is true.

"Hel-*lo*? Ground control to Major Loser," Sage says from the backseat, her voice bringing me to the present. "Why are you being such a space cadet tonight?"

"Shut up, Sage. I'm just focusing on the road." My hands clench the steering wheel.

"Are you, like, going out with Tate Brodeur?" Sierra asks.

"Are you, like, able to mind your own business?" My tone is a lot meaner than I want it to be. I just don't want to be the subject of the twins' gossip—I'm too vulnerable right now.

"What*ever*." I glance in the rearview mirror and see Sierra crossing her arms and sulking in the backseat. Sage pats her leg in reassurance.

"Jenny's probably just pissed off because *she* likes him but *he* doesn't feel the same way."

I turn my attention back to the road and grit my teeth. This is one of my biggest fears. But even so, another fear was added to the list tonight.

Not until I'm at home, safe in my room with the door all the way shut, in my old boxers and a well-worn T-shirt streaked with myriad paint colors, do I even say it out loud.

I might not be alone.

I look at the *Teen Vogue* article again, studying the facts about the Donor Sibling Registry and how it matches up donor offspring with their sisters and brothers, if possible. I realize now how big the *if* actually is. Who knows if my biological father, donor 142, made other donations at the same clinic my mom used? And even *if* he did, what are the odds of someone else picking it out, using it to get pregnant, and then having a baby? They seem pretty high to me for some reason. But just the fact that I *could* have more half siblings somewhere makes my stomach flip. I take the article into my closet and sit surrounded by tubes of paint, unfurled canvases, and paintbrushes of all sizes, hoping that somehow, being in here will help inspire me and I'll figure out what to do next.

I could just crawl into bed and go to sleep, but I already

know it's a lost cause. How could I sleep with thoughts like this fighting each other in my head? I could call Tate and talk to him about this, because I sure as hell can't call anyone else. Faye is stuck in cooking school jail. Russ would listen, but he'd probably feel weirded out at the thought that he might not be my only brother. Sierra and Sage are too young and annoying to get it. And my parents? Well, maybe my mom would understand, but my dad would feel rejected, I think. He might see my looking up info on the Donor Sibling Registry as slighting the family I already have, even though that couldn't be further from the truth.

If there's someone else out there genetically linked to me, it would just mean there's someone who exists, maybe even someone my age, with a strand of DNA that's linked forever to mine. This someone could be next door, or in the next town, or on the West Coast, or in another country. Regardless, that someone could be found with a few clicks of the mouse.

The thought of this being a reality gives me a visual. I grab a half-used tube of green so light it reminds me of the first tiny buds in spring. On a leftover piece of canvas, I use the nonbrush end of the paintbrush to make a thin, ragged line from one side to the other. In the middle of this arched brow, I twist my wrist to make an empty circle floating near the line of green, then another one. Two empty circles, not touching each other, not touching the line. Just floating together, side by side.

A knock on my door makes me jump. I'm easily surprised, so I've been the target of Russ's favorite practical joke since he was five, which is leaping out from behind a corner and screaming, "Jenny!" Faye says I need to accept spontaneity, but to me, whatever is lurking around the corner can be terrifying, even if it's familiar and you know it's coming.

Another knock on the door. I sigh as I put the paintbrush down and put Saran wrap around it so it won't dry out. So much for getting anywhere with a painting for the art show.

"Jenny?" My dad's voice filters through the door.

"Come in." I swing the door open with my toe and then go flop onto my bed.

"You okay?" he asks from the doorway.

I sit up and gaze at him. Maybe he can tell just by looking at me that my mind is racing. Dads tend to know these things instinctually. "Why do you ask?"

Dad comes in and rubs his hands together. He checks out the walls of my bedroom, the splattered painting on one side, the bright geometric canvas on the other. There's also a small watercolor of our house that I did a year ago. I cringe every time I see it, but honestly, I have no idea what to put in its place. "Thanks for taking the twins tonight." He continues to study my face for any sign of trouble. "I appreciate it."

"No problem." I'm trying not to sound as though my feelings are on a fast-spin cycle. "The mall wasn't so bad." I think of Tate's gorgeous eyes and a smile creeps across my face, but then just as quickly I think of the donor sibling Web site and the smile vanishes.

"Deep down Sierra and Sage appreciate the extra time you spend with them." He waits for me to agree. "They look up to you."

"I sincerely doubt that." I smirk and tuck my knees into my shirt, further stretching it out.

My dad sits next to me on the bed, and just when I think he's going to say something reassuring, like that Sage and Sierra will grow into their relationship with me, or that things will be better with them when they're older, he says, "What's that?"

He reaches for the *Teen Vogue* before I can stop him.

"Nothing," I say. "Just some light reading."

Dad stares at the cover. I wonder if he's glimpsed that bold orange headline, and if he has, what is going through his mind. "I didn't think you read fashion magazines."

"Sometimes I do." I take it back from him and toss it onto the floor like it means nothing to me. Maybe he didn't see it. Or maybe he did. I'm going to leave it to him to open the floor for discussion, just like always. I'm pretty sure he'll do what I expect him to do.

He pats my head and gives me a hug. "Good night, Jenny," he says. "Sleep well."

I should feel comforted by his predictability, but I'm not this time.

"You too."

Dad gets up and walks to the door. He pauses and turns around. I'm hoping he's going to surprise me here and say something encouraging about the art show or call me out on the article. "Hey, Jen? How about we finish that back-yard project this weekend? I'd love to get it done by the time school starts."

My heart falls. "Maybe, Dad. I might be busy."

"We can't put it off forever." He may as well be talking

about our relationship. If he's supposed to instinctually know what's wrong, how come he keeps suggesting these things we can do together—running, sports, yard work—and not comprehend that it's only pushing us farther apart?

When Dad shuffles off to bed, I take the few steps to my desk, turn on my computer, and wait. The familiar hum lulls me into my chair, and I type the address for the Donor Sibling Registry into the Web browser. My right hand rests on the mouse and I pull the cursor over to the login field. All I have to do is type in my info. I sit there, frozen with both panic and excitement. What if I find another branch of Donor 142's genetic family tree? What if I don't? Will I feel even more alone then?

I lift my hand from the mouse and, without debating further, shut down the computer. I bring my knees up to my chest and stare at the monitor's black screen, knowing that what's lurking around the corner will reveal itself eventually.

EIGHT

I spend the next day earning my studio time by fetching coffee for Sid Sleethly and the more accomplished artists at Downtown. I hope it'll take my mind off other things, but being surrounded by all these talented people makes me anxious about the art show. I just don't know if I have *it* in me, and if I do, I highly doubt that I will be able to discover it and create some sort of masterpiece in less than two weeks.

After his fifth cup of coffee, Sid would most likely agree with me.

"So you see, Jenny Fitzgerald," he says as he gestures to a giant rectangular canvas that takes up the better part of one of the washed concrete walls, "this is an example of *true* inspiration. The artist was able to properly convey the interior complexities and turn them outward into the visual medium."

I'm convinced he talks like this to make people think he's smarter than he is, or at least that he's not just a washed-up has-been. It's all I can do not to respond with sarcasm, so instead, I offer up this question in the hope he'll find it in his heart to help me. "In terms of the art show, though. Are you looking for something specific? I mean, is there a certain style you'd like to see, or am I just supposed to—"

He cuts me off with a hard glare from behind his dark-framed glasses. The look says it all—he dropped his heart somewhere back in New York City a decade ago. " 'Supposed to'? There's no *supposed to* in art. Dear God! How do you expect to create anything when you're out of touch with . . ." He mumbles to himself. He shakes his head and wanders off to bother someone far superior to me.

At this rate I'll be lucky to get him to even consider any of my paintings for the show, let alone display them. He's explained that slots are limited, and the goal of the show is to actually sell the work, not just exhibit it. I'd say my chances are like scoring a home run during a rain delay— impossible.

I tend to the next project at hand: cleaning up the mess that is the artists' lounge. When I think about it, Sid may have a shruken, prune-sized heart, but he has allowed me to become Downtown's prized indentured servant in lieu of charging me for studio time. But as I check out the number of empty coffee cans that are set to the side of the industrial sink and calculate how long it's going to take me to wash and dry each can so they can be filled with turpentine and cleaning agents, I go back to my original assumption—Sid is the Devil.

Before I attempt that task, I walk around the lounge and pick up crumpled balls of paper, stray pencils, and half-started sketches littering the ground. I collect signs that read THIS IS MY SANDWICH—DON'T TOUCH IT and IF THIS IS YOUR BRUSH, IT WON'T BE IF YOU KEEP LEAVING IT HERE and stack them on one side of the long communal table, where the artists share lunches, have meetings, and read art history books. The tabletop is coated with years of dried paints and goop. Sometimes I like to sit here and look at the swirls and pray for inspiration to hit me.

A dollop of yellow calls to mind the end of summer sun outside, and a streak of blue dotted with yellow looks like my eyes. I wonder if Tate noticed my eyes last night, just as I noticed his. I wonder if there is someone else out there whose eyes duplicate mine. Maybe it's because I envy Sierra and Sage, but in the hours I've thought about going to the Web site and seeing if I have a sibling match, I keep picturing finding a twin. Perhaps there's a brother living in California who has mottled blue eyes and loves licorice as much as I do. Or a girl like me who can't hit a ball to save her life but who has made money by sketching houses for holiday cards, as I once did.

"Are you going to sit and admire the scenery or actually earn your keep?" Sid oozes into the room with Jamaica Haas, a high-profile artist who has a studio in New York but uses Downtown when she's at her country cottage on the Connecticut shore one town away from Cutler. Despite the articles written about her in *Art Scene* and *Modern Works,* she's always been down-to-earth and nice to me.

"I was just taking a break." I reach over to a nearby bucket of water, fish out a large sponge, and begin wiping down the table so it gleams.

"If you keep scrubbing like that, your arms will fall off and Sid will be forced to sell them in the art show." Jamaica winks at me, and I smile. "You're Jenny, right?"

I nod and ignore Sid, who clearly wants me to evaporate so he can get back to schmoozing. "Yes. Jenny Fitzgerald. We met once before."

Jamaica fluffs out her dark funky bob. She looks like the human equivalent of a Scottish terrier—small and lively, with bright eyes and hair that sticks up. "You're the one who paints lots of circles."

"Yeah, I guess I just like them." I never thought that I had an artistic identity, but I love knowing that Jamaica thinks so.

"I guess I just like them." Sid Sleethly mimics me.

Obviously, he is not the Devil—he is the Devil's five-year-old son.

Jamaica takes the sponge from my hand and goes to the concrete wall. With a giant swooping motion, she makes a huge circle, then roughs the edges. "Well, I think you're onto something. Circles." She tilts her head and gazes at me like she knows something I don't. "I assume you'll have work at the art show?"

I look at Sid for confirmation of this, but he doesn't budge. "I'm hoping to."

"Well, I look forward to seeing it. Circles. Connection. Good stuff."

Blush tinges my cheeks as she and Sid head over to one of the couches. Her words stay with me minutes later when I sneak off to my own canvas and use a pencil to outline my ideas. But I stand there for hours, and when I leave to pick up the twins from Camp Cedar, the canvas is still bright white and stark.

"Ohmygodyouwillikeneverbelievethis." Sierra talks so fast when she's excited that I have to decipher each word. Sage, on the other hand, responds to excitement on slo-mo, so she stands by the car with her mouth hanging open.

Sierra clutches Sage's arm. Their skin is the exact same tone; they are connected like paper dolls with seamless limbs.

"What's going on?" I get out of the car and scan the parking lot for Tate. I have that big crush feeling where I'm half-wishing he'll notice me again and half-hoping he won't. In this case it doesn't appear to matter what I wish, because everywhere I look, there is no Tate.

Sierra is bouncing up and down in her leotard while Sage stays grounded. "Checkitoutohmygodohmygod! We qualified!"

"Qualified for what?" Maybe she means for some eighth-grade team or some after-school program. "Are you taking an advanced class or something? Throw your bags in the back."

Sierra and Sage stop clutching each other long enough to, for once, clutch my arm. "We both qualified for the Dance Project. It's this amazing recital featuring—"

"I know," I interrupt, not thinking for a second that maybe I should let them continue to share their news. "I read about it in the paper. An urban dance troupe that tours the United States. Very cool!" Really, I am psyched for them. It's a big deal, especially for girls their age. So why do I feel like my congratulations are semi-hollow?

Sierra and Sage look at each other and drop their hold on my arm. They've picked up on it too. "You don't seem that happy for us," Sage says, and opens the car door. Sierra crawls into the backseat after her.

"Of course I'm happy for you!" I lean over and pop my head into the backseat before shutting the door. "Seriously, I'm so proud of you guys."

They perk up a bit at hearing this, and it stings knowing that they never, ever say things like that to me. It's strange— I keeping feeling as though I wish someone were here holding my hand, but I don't know if that person is Tate or a half sibling. Either way, it's as though I'm wishing for something that will only be a dream.

I get in the car and turn the key in the ignition. Sierra leans forward between the front seats so she can switch the radio to her and Sage's favorite station. "You don't mind, do you?"

It's not worth arguing over. Two against one always wins.

"Hey, Jenny!" Sage rummages around in her bag for something. "I almost forgot."

"Oh yeah, you need to give her the thing!" Sierra squeals.

"What is it?" I peer at them in the rearview mirror. "Another trophy? A medal? A gymnastics award?"

"No, there are too many of those to carry around," Sage jokes.

A folded-up piece of paper flies out from the backseat and onto the dashboard.

I don't have to open the folded piece of graph paper to recognize the handwriting. It's a note from Tate Brodeur.

I think about reading it when I get to the safety of my room—that way the twins can't try and sneak a peek at it—but I don't have an ounce of patience.

I read each slanted letter with bated breath.

Hey JF—
  Can't take the suspense, so end the torture
  already. Did you check the site? Circle Yes or No.
                  Inquisitively, TB

When I fold the note back up and put it in my left pocket, I remind myself that this definitely isn't a dream.

NINE

An hour later I'm on my bed, rereading Tate's note for the fifth time.

Yes or no? To circle or not to circle? I can't help but fantasize about whether there's some hidden meaning in this question, like he's asking me if I'd like to be his girlfriend. But this piece of info is still another unknown entity, waiting to jump out at me from around an invisible corner.

My door opens without a knock. Sage is there in pounce mode. "Time for dinner." She rolls her eyes when she sees what I'm reading. "Omigod, Jenny, could you be any lamer?"

"Could you be any more of a pain in my ass?" I jab at her. "Try knocking sometime. It's the polite thing to do."

"Like you even need privacy," she laughs.

Sierra suddenly appears. Sage must have summoned her telepathically. "Maybe we should leave Jenny alone so she can check out certain Web sites . . ."

I reach behind me, grab a pillow, and throw it at them. "I can't believe you read my letter."

Sage and Sierra just snicker and are on their merry way.

I drag myself off my bed and into the hall. The twins are trotting ahead of me. As we come down the stairs, I can hear my parents discussing the pros and cons of setting up some sort of an obstacle course in our backyard, complete with swinging ropes and tires on the ground. That's just what I need—another reminder of how uncoordinated I am in the family realm.

Sierra and Sage go into the kitchen to help Mom. I turn the corner to the living room, and suddenly Russ leaps out and shouts, "Jenny!"

I gasp and clutch at my heart.

Russ laughs. "Wow. That never gets old."

"You suck, you know that?"

"Yes, I know," he says, grinning. "So, Sierra and Sage told me there's some Web site you want me to see."

I resolve to berate the twins after dinner.

"Just ignore them, Russ," I groan.

He squints at me. "What's wrong?"

I shrug and frown. "Nothing." A part of me wishes I could confide in him. But I can't.

"Whatever you say." Russ stretches, bringing one arm in front of him and pulling on it with the other. Then he runs his hand through his hair. He's looking more like Dad every day. I don't know how I feel about sharing the hallways with him at County High School this fall. "Jenny?"

"Yeah?"

"Bro's a good guy."

"Who?"

"Tate, genius." Russ stretches the other arm. "I'm just saying, I wouldn't worry if I were you."

Even though Russ only guessed at half of what's bothering me, I've never felt more like his full sister than I do now.

The Fitzgerald family sits down at the dining room table while Mom brings out the main course. She puts a plate filled with lamb chops and mashed potatoes in front of me while patting my hair. I brush her hand off my head and then feel bad that I did it, but when I reach up to put her hand back, she's already moved on.

"Did you hear the good news?" Dad asks. He's fresh from a jog, with ruddy cheeks and drips of perspiration running from his thinning hairline. He loves to run through the wooded trails near the house all year long, even in the snow.

"That you're going to shower soon?" Russ jokes.

Dad smirks. "No. Although, I'm sure that'd be exciting news for everyone."

Mom takes over. "The twins qualified for the Dance Project!"

I nod, overly emphatic in order to seem superpsyched. "I know."

"It'll be a family event," Dad says. "We'll all go and see the show and then celebrate in town."

"I'll make reservations," Mom agrees.

"Awesome," Russ says with his mouth full. He locks eyes with me as he chews.

I think he's trying to tell me something, but since we don't have that twin-connection thing, whatever is on his mind remains a mystery to me.

"I actually have to run," I say, my appetite gone.

"More painting?" my mom asks. Dad waits for my answer, probably hoping that I'll say I have converted from the religion of art to sports fanaticism.

"Not tonight," I say. "I have other things to work on."

After dinner I dash upstairs to my room and dial Tate's number, which I have already managed to memorize. As I stare at the numbers, I find myself fixating on the one, then the four, then the two: 142. The donor number. *My* donor number. I should find out if it's anyone else's. The thing is, I feel as if it's not a decision anymore. It's a necessity.

Tate's voice echoes in my ear. "Jenny?"

I grin when I hear him say my name. "How'd you guess?"

"I know I should say something cool like I had a feeling it'd be you, but of course, I have to thank caller ID."

"Too bad. I thought we were psychically connected." Then I worry I said too much.

"Nope, not at present. But we could work on that."

I hope he means we *will* work on that. Oh my God, I *have* to stop overanalyzing. "So . . ."

"So . . . ," he says. "Did you do it?"

Even though it's juvenile, whenever I hear *do it* I think about sex and how I haven't done much and how I wonder if that's obvious to everyone who looks at me.

"You know, do you have a brother somewhere? Aside from Russ, I mean. Man, can you imagine if you did, and he was as fast as Russ? We'd have to import him for County." Tate stops himself, either afraid of sounding too jocky or, more likely, not wanting to assume that I found anyone at all.

"Ah, the Registry." I shake my head as if he can see the gesture and then slap my forehead. "I'm afraid I don't have much to tell you. I didn't even log on."

"Well, that's okay. I really wanted you to call me, no matter what happened."

Cue heart racing. I stare at the watercolor painting I made of our house and imagine what his house looks like and if I'll ever get to see it.

Someone taps at the door. "Jenny, it's your turn to do dishes." Ugh. Dad.

"Hold on a sec," I say to Tate and then cover the mouthpiece of the phone. I don't know why I'm about to do this, because I know what's going to happen. "Can you ask Russ to do them? I'm busy."

"Now, Jenny."

End of discussion.

"I have to go," I tell Tate. I worry that it sounds lame, as if I don't want to keep talking, which of course I do. Quite honestly, I'd be happy just hearing him breathe into the phone.

"You had to go pretty quickly last night, too," Tate replies. "I get it. No problem."

His tone has changed and slipped into that guy-friend voice. I know the phrase *see you around* is next in line if I don't say something. "Wait, I want to keep talking. I do. But I can't."

"Can't now or can't ever?"

Tate's questions challenge me. I really like that about him. "I just have dishes to wash."

An awkward silence is followed by, "So . . . ?"

"So . . . ?" I counter.

"Want to come over later?" he asks.

For once the loud thud I hear isn't a ball hitting the side of the house; it's my heart caving in. I try to sound easygoing and mellow, but my words still come out overtly happy. He has said what I have wanted to hear for so long. "Sure! That'd be great! I'll see you in an hour or so?"

I start to hang up the phone, but Tate is still talking. "Don't you need my address?"

"Oh, right," I say, even though I know it. I forget how I may have gotten that information, which leads me to believe that I've always known it.

"One-forty-one Wellesley Street, off Marchese," he says. "See you in a while. Yes?"

"Yes."

It only occurs to me when I pull up in front of his house that 141 is one number shy of 142. Maybe Tate will help me make up the difference.

TEN

One of the things I like best about art is that the line between reality and fantasy always blurs. Even with paintings
such as Paul Cézanne's *Still Life with a Ginger Jar and
Eggplants,* the viewer can't determine whether the painter
was just copying the objects or making them better—the
eggplants darker, fuller; the jar cleaner, glinting with life.

This is how I feel when I get to Tate's house, with
BRODEUR and 141 displayed on tiles set into the stone wall
surrounding the front walkway. My fantasy for the past
two years has been that he'd ask me over, that I'd go, and
that I'd somehow look ravishing even in my plain old dark
green T-shirt that only has one small dot of paint at the
waist hem. Tate would open the door and look at me, and
without having to say anything, he'd take me in his arms
and kiss me. My reality isn't quite the same, but who's to
say which is better?

"Hey, Fitz," he says as soon as he opens the door. No one
ever calls me Fitz, probably because I don't play sports. I'm
not sure how to take it, but it doesn't bug me like it might

have coming from my parents or Russ. He looks amazing, greeting me with a grin and a hand that motions for me to follow him inside.

"Great house," I say. Then, just in case I sound superficial (because isn't it a total cliché to go to someone's house for the first time and compliment it right when you come in?), I add, "The light is perfect for painting."

Tate shrugs, not in a disinterested way, but in a *never thought of that* way. "Well, anytime you feel like it, just show up with a canvas and a brush."

"I just might take you up on that offer. I could set up right here." I stomp my feet right in the center of the airy entryway and pretend to dip a paintbrush into a pot of paint.

"I have a better idea."

Tate leads me up the stairs to the hallway that I assume leads to the bedrooms. My pulse races and I take a breath. "Where're we going?"

"You'll see," he says.

"Isn't that what the killer says in horror movies, right before he does something terrible?" I ask, forcing a smile. What if he stops on the stairs and kisses me? What if he leads me to his bedroom and wants to give me a tour of his, um, bed? What if nothing happens at all?

"Close your eyes," Tate commands. I obey and then don't. "Close them!" he says again.

I cross my arms over my chest. "Why?"

"It's a surprise," he explains.

"I don't like surprises," I fire back. There's a cynical expression on his face—he doesn't buy it. "Really. My sweet sixteen birthday party was a disaster. My whole family and all my friends jumped out from behind the furniture and I practically died from shock. I had to be rushed to the hospital. I was there for *days*!"

Tate laughs. "Okay, okay. I got it. No surprises." He moves toward me so we're maybe a foot away from each other in the hallway outside a closed door. The lighting is calm, like near paintings in a museum. His eyes focus on mine, then move to my lips. Faye read in an article that if a guy looks at your lips when he's talking to you, it means he's thinking about kissing you. My, oh my.

"Good. I'm glad we got that settled." I don't move, so I can keep trying to read his eyes. "No surprises."

Tate moves toward me even more. He's going to put his arms around my waist. He's going to pull me close to him. He's going to . . . open the door. Oh. "Go on in," he says, and swings the door open, revealing a set of narrow stairs.

I climb the steps two at a time, holding the polished wooden railing for balance. When I reach the last step, I take a deep breath. Not because I'm out of shape and out of breath, but because it's so cool.

"This is awesome!" I say. "In the real sense, not the, like, overly used *awesome* in a cheerleader sense." Then I blush. He's actually friends with that crowd.

"I like that distinction." Tate's smile completely floors me.

We are standing in a small room shaped in a hexagon. All the walls are windows, or the windows are walls, whichever. "I feel like I'm outside, even though I'm not." I go over to one of the window/walls and peer out into the dusky sky. It's just like Tate to challenge my perspective like this. I'm a little dizzy, probably because Tate is standing mere inches away.

"I love this place," he says. "My parents never come up here. Then again, they're never home to begin with."

There's silence. Outside, the wind shifts through the trees, and feeling Tate's eyes on me makes my legs want to give way. I try to ground myself by looking at the red splotch of paint at the hem of my shirt. "It's definitely a cool room," I say.

"Yeah, it is," Tate agrees.

I'm so busy picking at the paint drip, staring at the odd shape of it so I can avoid staring at this guy, this person whom I've wanted for so long, that I don't realize quite how close to me he's standing until he taps me on the shoulder and I look up. We're less than a paintbrush length apart. There's no doubt in my mind he's going to kiss me. But I'm wrong, because all he does is look at me, raise his eyebrows, and ask, "Ready to go downstairs?"

Tate bounds down the steps first, and I watch his easy stride, taking note of the way his waffle shirt is half tucked into his jeans. Painted images of gray waves come to mind and then stop. Tate halts himself and suddenly, in one fluid motion, turns around on the stairs, moves both arms so one hand is around my waist and the other palms the back of my head, and pulls me close. I am one step above him. Tate has made up the difference all right—the difference between our heights—so we're eye to eye now. My heart is having convulsions. It's like when Russ tries to surprise-scare me—it's as if I couldn't have expected this, and yet should have all along.

Tate puts his mouth on mine and we kiss slowly. His lips are just the right amount moist without being slobbery, and he tastes even better than red licorice. When I pull back, Tate's eyes are still closed, and when he opens them, a wide grin forms on his face. I'm smiling at him so hard, I think I might have pulled a muscle in my cheek.

"How do you feel about surprises now?" he asks coyly.

I feel chills spreading from my neck, where Tate's fingers are tucked into my hair, down to my thighs. "Maybe I should reconsider them." Then I kiss him again. It's even better than the last one because *I* went in for the kiss and he's kissing me back, reciprocating. I want to tell him how long I've waited for this, but I don't.

Instead, Tate takes my hand and leads me down the stairs and back to the kitchen. "Can I tell you that I've wanted to do that for a long time, without sounding like a stalker?"

"Define 'long time.'" I hoist myself up on the counter next to a bowl of fruit. I could paint a still life of the piled pears, the bright oranges, and it would never compare to the reality of right now.

Tate sighs and gets us both a glass of fancy Italian soda from a bottle with a built-in cork. "Let's just say long enough." He smiles and then thinks of something. "Last night at the mall only confirmed my suspicions."

I sip the drink, and Tate steps in between my knees so his face is level with mine. It's a kissing position big with the cheerleaders and their jock boyfriends at school. I guess it's because the girls can sit on the bleachers and their sporty guys can hustle over in between sprints. But I'm not in that crowd and never will be. Nerves kick in momentarily. Two weeks left of summer and then what? Will we fall back into our separate worlds? But I'm getting way ahead of myself. "What suspicions were those?"

Tate shrugs. "That you were funny. Different, in a good way. Unique."

I smile. "Oh." It's hard to know what else to say when someone rattles off a list of qualities you can only hope to have. Now's the time I could express exactly what I feel. Only, what is it? Finding the right words to express how you feel about someone is so easy at night, alone in your bed with only the slim blue light from the summer sky as witness. How many times have I thought about what I'd say to Tate Brodeur if given the chance? And here, now, when the moment's in front of me, I come up with "Oh." Luckily, Tate's not at a loss for words.

"Smart, which I knew from being in class with you. And . . ." He looks me up and down. "Absolutely stunning."

No one has ever called me this before. Not even close. It makes my head spin, but then Tate goes on. "Which is why when I saw that article last night . . ." He walks away for a second, making me miss him already, and then comes back with the magazine. "Here's the thing. You're everything I said before, right?"

"That's a trick question. If I say yes, then I'm conceited, and if I say no, then I lack self-confidence."

Tate's grin goes wide. "Classic. Anyway, I just keep thinking, if you're so cool, what if there's someone else out there like you? That's got to be a good thing."

As soon as he says it, as soon as the words are out of his

mouth, hovering in the air like monarch butterflies with their vibrant orange-and-black wings, I know he's right. I have to know. Just like I knew I had to kiss Tate. To confirm the feeling, I say it aloud. "I have to know."

Tate claps his hands like we're about to *hut, hut, hike* or something. "Good. I'm so glad you're doing this. The suspense was really getting to me."

I raise my eyebrows as he wanders over to the small office next to the kitchen, sits down at a desk, and fires up a laptop. "Oh, *you* were anxious?" I say. "Please." I hop off the counter, follow him into the room, and take a seat next to him so we're side by side.

"Sorry, you're right. If I feel stressed about this, you must feel . . ."

"Bombarded with crazy," I say. Slowly, deliberately, I type in the Web address for the Donor Sibling Registry. "It's like it shouldn't be so colossal, but it is. I mean, maybe there's no one. But maybe there's . . ." I stop talking when the site appears in front of me.

"Whenever you're ready," Tate says, putting his hand on my knee.

"Okay." I take a deep breath and hold the mouse. "I'm ready."

ELEVEN

Scrolling around the site isn't as scary as I thought it would be. No one ambushes me and announces they're related, which is a little bit of a relief. It's funny how Tate seems more anxious than I am. He's tapping his sneaker-clad feet on the chair rung. I fire an irritated look at him and he winces.

"Sorry, this is nerve-racking. Can't you just type something in and get a match?"

"If it were that simple, I would've done it already." I bite my top lip. "I'm going to do a search of the bank my mom used." Note how I left out the word *sperm*. I just don't feel the need to mention that in front of my new boyfriend. If that's what he actually is.

Tate watches intently, his arms crossed over his chest like this is the championship cup or match. "Isn't California Reproductive Center one of the biggest in the country?"

"I think so." I squint at the screen as I continue to type.

Afterward, I click the mouse. "Oh my God." I rub my hands together, unsure what to do.

"What? What is it?"

"I don't know. There are a couple of postings here." I frantically scan the screen for important details. I read the first posting to Tate, my voice wavering slightly. "This one's color-coded blue, which means . . ." I quickly check the color key. "It was posted by the donor."

Tate scoots closer to me. "Maybe it's your father."

For some reason, I'm overcome with emotion and tears well up in my eyes. "My dad's at home, digesting a pile of mashed potatoes and watching Sierra and Sage practice their dance moves."

"Of course. You're right. I didn't mean to be insensitive."

I pat his thigh, my hand on his bare leg. "It's okay." I click on the posting. "This man says he's of Scottish descent. Hey, maybe I'm Scottish!" An image of me in a kilt appears in my head and then fades as I read. "He started donating in the early nineties. Wow, that's pretty close, time-wise." I keep reading. "He's six feet, two inches tall." My hopes rise and then fall way down when I read the rest of the entry. "Forget it. He's African American."

Tate points to the screen. "What about that one?"

I read carefully. "Interesting. It's a different color posting, one that means it's from parents who are searching on behalf of their child."

"And?"

"They have a daughter who was born the same year I

was." My eyes travel the length of the short entry, reading the name of the clinic they went to. Then I shout, "One-four-two! That's my donor father's number! And it's her father's number, too." The world seems to collapse and get smaller, then just as quickly unfold and expand, stretching like a blot of oil paint dripped on a canvas. "I think I found a sister."

"Holy shit," Tate says. Then he puts his hand to his mouth. "Sorry."

I laugh. "Don't be sorry. I think that reaction was completely appropriate."

"So now what?"

I sigh and sit back in the chair. There are so many answers to this question. I could wait. I could let all this info sink in and think on it tonight or tomorrow while trying to paint. I could call my parents, or I could walk around not knowing. But that's cowardly, isn't it? I'm so mixed up inside that all I can say is, "I don't know."

"Do you want me to leave you alone for a minute?" Tate asks. He so gets it, gets me. I nod.

"Thanks."

"I'll go make us some dessert. I'm known for creating strange but delicious milkshakes."

"Sounds good." I watch him exit into the kitchen, and although he does leave me alone, I feel connected to a presence elsewhere, kind of like how twins often say that they can feel when their twin is hurt or happy.

I register online and pay the fee with my bank card's direct debit, and then go back to the 142 match and click.

The site warns about possible mismatches, but somehow, deep down, I know I don't need to worry about that.

> *Our daughter, Alexa, is looking for any matches. She has an e-mail account set up specifically for this purpose. If you believe you are a match, please e-mail couldyoubethe-match@yahoo.com with your information and Alexa will get back to you as soon as she can.*

What do I write to my possibly-maybe half sister Alexa? If only I could paint a picture, it would show me as this dot of blue in the corner, and then have arching lines out to another dot of a different color in another corner. I grab a scrap of paper and sketch this out, just so I have it for tomorrow. Who knows? Perhaps I'll actually paint something.

"How's it going in there?" Tate yells from the kitchen. I can hear drawers opening and the fast whir of a blender. Tate Brodeur is making me a milkshake. Tate Brodeur kissed me tonight. Tate Brodeur was there when I clicked and found her.

> *Dear Alexa,*
> *I don't know how to start this letter, but I guess in writing that, I have. I think you and I are related—that is, I think we have the same donor father, number 142 from the California Reproductive Center. I was born the same year you were, out in California, but now I live*

I pause. I don't want to give away too much private info, just in case. I remember my parents and their repeated warnings about being careful on the Internet. I continue pounding on the keyboard.

on the East Coast with my parents and siblings.
I really want to know if we're a true match, so
please e-mail ASAP.
                                                    —Jenny F.

I don't tell her my likes and dislikes, my taste in music, or that I love to paint. It sounds too much like the personal ads at the back of the newspaper that Faye and I read aloud, joking about how lame they are. Instead, I just click and send the e-mail before I can edit myself.

Once I hit the send button, I feel a wave of peacefulness wash over me, which heightens when Tate calls out to me to join him in the kitchen.

"Vanilla, black raspberry, chocolate mint!" he yells to me. "It sounds kind of gross, but it's awesome."

I rise from the chair and turn off the computer. I'm ready to taste whatever it is Tate (my boyfriend? My friend? My something) has churned up in the blender and to face whatever happens—or doesn't—with Alexa (my half sister? My something? Or nothing?).

TWELVE

I spend the next day running up and down the stairs, checking my e-mail so frequently that not only do I start to wear
a tread on the carpet, but my parents intervene.

"Is something wrong?" my mother asks while paging
through bills and writing checks at the kitchen table. The
sprinkler hisses outside, where my father stands with his
hands on his hips as though he's about to lecture the lawn
on its shoddy behavior.

"No, not at all." I swig back some orange juice mixed
with seltzer water and wonder—again—if my account has
any new messages.

"How's the artwork coming along?" Mom looks up, pen
in hand, and gives me her interested look. I notice she furrows her brow and does the tiniest of nods when she tries to
convey just how much she's listening. "The big show is after the carnival, right?

"Yeah, the day after," I mumble. Every summer a travel-
ing carnival comes to our town, bringing cotton candy,
dunking tanks and other game booths where people like me

who can't throw are constantly humiliated, and rides that make your head and belly spin. Couples always make out on the top of the Ferris wheel, and last year some kid barfed on my shoes, which wouldn't have been so bad except I was wearing sandals. I hope this year is better. But it won't be if I can't be a part of the art show afterward.

"I'm having trouble, actually." I sit down at the table and rest my arms on the top of it. I think about telling her what happened last night, but when I study her face and think of how my own might look more like Alexa's than hers, I don't. "Why is it that I can easily think of images in my head, but when I try to transfer them onto the page, or canvas, they either disappear or don't seem as great as they did before?"

My mother puts her pen down and exhales through her nose. "When I was doing film ages ago, people used to say if something isn't right on the page, it isn't right, period. So maybe it isn't the translation process, but the image you have." She licks an envelope and seals it shut with her palm. "Maybe your preconceived notions about what *should* be, or what *could* be, are blocking what actually *is*. Does that make sense?"

I nod and finish my drink. She's more insightful than I give her credit for sometimes. "It does. Thanks, Mom."

"Are you going to the studio today?"

"Yeah, a little later. On Saturdays they have afternoon and evening hours, so I won't be here for dinner."

"Oh, that's too bad," she says. "The girls are doing a whole run-through of their dance routine."

A twinge of annoyance rumbles in my chest. "So I'm supposed to not go to work so I can watch them practice?"

My mother sounds exasperated. "I never said that. I only meant that it would be nice for you to see them. They're working hard."

Blush creeps up my cheeks. "We all work hard!" I say tersely. My dad uses this line during counseling sessions when mediating couples bicker over who carries more weight in their marriage. Dad always says that using the plural *we* makes people less defensive, like we're all in it together, rather than every person for himself or herself. Then again, I'm defensive enough for both of us right now. "Not that anyone cares what kind of work I'm doing."

I know I'm overreacting—she did just ask how my work was going, after all, but the truth is, I want someone to make reservations at some nice place in town for dinner after the art show like they have for the twins. I hate feeling as if I'm competing for affection, which is why I don't give her a chance to reassure me and instead run upstairs to my room and check my e-mail.

Before I sit in front of my desktop computer, I see a scrap of paper on my desk and unfold it. I stare at the sketch I made last night at Tate's. Two dots connected by lines. It's not much, but it's something. I always think inspiration should knock you over or belt you out of sleep, but maybe it just taps you politely on the shoulder and it's up to you to make the most of it.

So I do. In the haven of my closet, I take my good set of paints and squeeze various tubes so the colors dot my egg crate palette: Naples yellow, Venetian red, bright white, terra-cotta. Using cobalt blue, I sweep a line from corner to corner on the rectangular canvas, eschewing my usual paper and pencil sketch.

Maybe my problem is that I practice too much. My family is so big on practicing because it works for learning plays or choreographing a dance. But for painting maybe it's best not to overthink.

The colors, the textures, the finishes of the paints lure me further into this world I'm creating. On the far left side is a deep green dot with edges I've feathered so it looks soft, pliant. Then on the lower right corner is the cobalt dot, with more defined edges. Connecting them are washes and lines of other colors, so that overlap and definitions blend.

I only stop when I hear the telltale sound of my door opening. "Did I say you could come in?" I refuse to divert my eyes from the canvas. Whoever it is should hear the sarcasm in my voice and then leave.

"Can I?"

I spin around and see Tate. His hands are shoved into his pockets and his eyes are bright as he grins. "I thought you were my sisters. They come in unannounced all the time."

Tate forgives me for snapping at him and walks into the closet with me. As he leans in toward me, I'm wondering if he has forgotten about last night and is about to give me a platonic cheek smooch. Instead, he deposits a kiss firmly on my mouth. Afterward, as he turns his attention to my canvas, the taste of him still lingers on my lips.

"This is cool. I like the shading over here. Very Turneresque."

My mouth twists into a big grin. I'm starting to think if I don't hear from Alexa, there might be someone else who could completely understand me. "Yeah, it is. But I'm not trying to imitate Turner, of course."

"Of course not."

I pick up a tube of paint and fidget nervously with it. "I want to make it even more seamless, but I haven't figured out how."

"You will," Tate says confidently.

He shuffles out of the closet and plops down on my bed. It seems hard to imagine the nights I lay right there on those sheets, wishing for him to notice me, and in one steady rush, everything I thought about happened. Granted, it took two years of crushing, many sleepless nights of longing, and countless hours of interest from a distance, but here he is, in my room.

"Want to meet me at Callahan's later?" He's spread out on my old beige comforter. Last Christmas my mom got me a geometric-patterned cover for my bed, which I have never used. So many colors swirl in my mind that I need my bed to be a a place of calm, and design-free. The twins have said more than once that my bed linens "lack character," though I know for a fact they cribbed that phrase from their gymnastics coach, who threw the same line at me when I was a kid and attempted (for one crappy fall) to do a floor routine.

Tate sits up and looks at me expectantly. "Some of the guys and I are meeting there. I'd love it if you hung out with us."

Us equals the sporty guys and their chain-linked girl-friends. A wisp of anxiety takes hold of me. "I have to work this afternoon."

"Well, what about after work?"

I clear my throat and start cleaning up the paints, sticking the brushes into baby food jars filled with paint thinner, wiping my hands on a rag. The stench of oil paint and chemicals fills my nose and makes me light-headed, so I leave the closet and stand in front of Tate. "I actually have to be at the studio until closing time."

"So forget Cally's. How about I meet you there? When you're on your break, of course."

I perk up. I don't have to deal with the mall scene, but I still get to see Tate. I like this plan. "Ring the top buzzer at nine. I'll let you in."

We hug good-bye and I relish the feel of him near me. When I look up at him, his eyes are closed and he's breathing deeply. All I can think is, *Yum.* He squeezes me one more time for emphasis and then breaks away. "See you soon."

I nod and watch him dart out of the room. As I'm standing there, I catch a glimpse of myself in the mirror on the back of my wall. The door is still closed halfway, so I can't see all of me, just one leg, one arm, one side of my face and body. Evidence of my work in the closet shows on my brow—cobalt smears here, speckles of green there. I like that I can't see the other side of me, like it exists elsewhere.

Suddenly a *blurp* comes from my computer. It's a reminder for an unanswered instant message. I'm hoping Faye has conned the head chef into letting her use the cooking school's lone computer. I can't wait to talk to her, so I rush over, sit my paint-free butt in the chair, and click on the blinking bar at the bottom of the screen.

U there Jenny F? It's me, Alexa

Oh my God. Alexa. I answer immediately, the dried paint on my knuckles cracking as I type.

Hi Alexa! How'd you get my IM?

Seconds after I send my reply, another one pops up.

Wouldn't you like to know ;-)

I smile. The girl has a sense of humor.

There are more important things I'd like to know, actually ☺

I stare at the blinking cursor until she replies.

Tell me about it! We could be sisters!

We then proceed to have a marathon of IMs all sent overlapping and rushed, filled with questions and concerns. Every cell in my body is racing, speeding like those fast-forwarded scenes in movies of traffic at night: alive, and moving ahead.

JennyFitz2Paint: So why did you post that message on the DSR?

AlexaMC: In this giant universe I knew there had to be someone out there who was a match.

JennyFitz2Paint: But are we really?

I wait for a second while she types, wondering what she'll say.

AlexaMC: I HAVE A GOOD FEELING! IN FACT I AM SO EXCITED I HAVE TO TYPE IN ALL CAPS!!

We go over every scrap of evidence: the clinic name, the year, my mom and her location. I wish we were on the phone, because then I'd hear her voice, but as we type I can envision her anyway. By the way she's jutting in while I'm still writing, I can tell that she is intense and has a lot of energy. In fact, I can barely keep up with her.

AlexaMC: My moms (no, not a typo, I have 2) are reading this BTW, because they are all about Internet safety, blah blah blah.

JennyFitz2Paint: I understand. So what comes next?

My IM window stays still and unblinking for a full three minutes while I pick at the paint on my face.

AlexaMC: Hi.

JennyFitz2Paint: Hi back.

I bring my legs up to my chest and wrap my arms around them. I'm bracing myself for whatever she types back.

AlexaMC: My moms say we're a match! Can u believe it? We're SISTERS!!

I feel as if I'm in a dream, floating high above the ground, both excited and scared when I look down below. My fingers shake as I begin to type a response, but Alexa has already beat me to the punch.

AlexaMC: So when do we get to meet?

THIRTEEN

For the rest of the day I keep thinking of those words, *we're a match*. All this time, I have watched the way Sierra and Sage have effortlessly coexisted, and now I have a match of my own. I know Alexa Mason-Cohen and I are only half sisters, so our genes aren't a total mesh, but I can't help but believe she's the piece that I've felt I was lacking this whole time.

Still, I'm not ready to jump into our shared gene pool and meet her. There's too much going on in my life as it is. School starts soon. The art show is even sooner—Sunday, September 5, from 4 p.m. until 7 p.m., to be exact. I'm tangled up with Tate and have no idea where that will lead.

I've been working at the studios for hours on the rectangular painting I started earlier in my closet, only I've started fresh on the canvas I sketched on before. I erased the arcing line with an industrial-sized eraser and have, once again, a clean canvas that's ready for anything. The only trouble is, I don't know what to put on it, and even if I did, I can barely concentrate because now I'm thinking about these words: *So when do we get to meet?*

If this keeps up, there will be no chance in hell I will have anything ready for the art show.

"Picasso once wrote that painting is just another way of keeping a diary."

I turn to see Jamaica Haas, dressed in lilac from scarf to sandals, with long, tubular yellow earrings. She looks so artsy and beautiful, almost like an iris. I'm almost ashamed of my paint-splattered clothing and facial smears.

"Well, if this is my diary, it's appalling," I say, and turn back to the empty canvas.

"That's highly critical." She steps into my cubby space so she can peer at the tubes of paint. "You know, sometimes when I have a void, I just fill it with whatever words come to mind. Only I don't paint words, I paint them as images. Otherwise, I'd be a poet, and my writing skills are paltry at best."

She slides out of the room as easily as she entered, leaving me with only her advice as company. Then it hits me. We're a match.

I close my eyes and picture what these words would look like if they weren't words. And then I start to paint.

An hour or so later, I buzz Tate up and give him a tour of Downtown, culminating with my painting, which is still pretty wet.

"You did all this tonight?" he asks.

"Yeah. I don't know what happened!" I gush. It's been forever since I was able to paint something fluidly, without stopping to examine every inch. "And I don't hate it, which is also a near first."

Tate nods in affirmation. "I know what you mean. After games I'm always dissecting my plays, what I did, what went wrong, where I can improve. I'm my own coach-slash-critic."

I lean on the cool concrete wall and look at the bright magenta hues that combust with vibrant oranges and result in a painting that (to me, anyway) is about matching, with two sides of the canvas that meet in the middle. Tate puts a hand on the wall behind me so his face is close to mine. He is about to kiss me when a painting comes half unhinged and threatens to fall.

I jump up, put it back on the hook, and try to resume the prekiss position with Tate. He leans in but doesn't kiss me. I stifle a laugh.

Tate gives me a confused look. "What's so funny?"

"Nothing. I'm just thinking how weird it is that we're here." I don't know how to explain what I mean, and I'm sure Tate will ask.

Tate smirks. "What does that mean?"

Bingo.

I tilt my head up, looking at his full lips and then at his eyes, all swirls of green and blue, rings of rivers. "Let me put it this way. Aren't your friends going to laugh when you tell them you came here to meet me?"

Tate props himself up on both hands like he's going to do

a push-up against the wall. After he descends slowly, he lets his lips touch mine lightly. "I couldn't care less about what they think."

This should put me at ease, but it doesn't. Right now we are in that amazing summer space where nothing feels permanent. At some point we have to go back to school, and in school Tate and I don't effortlessly coexist. I can feel panic building within me, especially because I can't stop thinking about Alexa and the possibility of meeting her in person. Just as I'm about to spill my guts to Tate, Sid slithers into the room and groans loudly.

"Is there anything more clichéd than teenage lust?" He clomps over to us in his black boots, which are so out of season, and stares at my painting while I try to ignore the fact that he's just seen Tate and me kissing. "So, this is the latest?" Sid whistles through his teeth. It's a sound so high-pitched and grating even the paint threatens to peel off.

I try to remain calm in the face of impending criticism and find myself shifting into defensive mode. A part of me wonders, if Alexa were here would she leap to my rescue and tell him off? "It's just a start. I've only been working on it for one day and—"

"Rule one of being an artist," Sid interrupts, nearly spitting on the canvas. Tate looks at me as though he wants to intervene, but I shake my head. "Do not, under any circumstances, defend your work. If the audience doesn't respond, either find a new direction or accept their reaction as a result of their being uninformed."

I consider this for a second. "So if someone doesn't like my stuff, then it's their fault?"

"Yes."

"So if I follow that rule, then I can disregard all the times this summer you've said my work is terrible and blame it on you?"

From the doorway Jamaica Haas and another artist, a guy with high-tops and wire-rimmed glasses, laugh as they pass by. Sid seethes but smiles through closed lips. "No. When I'm referring to your work this summer, you can disregard rule one and go to rule two: amateurs are always amateurs."

I don't even know why I want Sid to like my work. He is obviously Satan.

"Well, I'm sorry about being such an amateur." I wipe my hands on a rag. All of a sudden Tate does something wonderful. He takes the rag out of my hand and shoves it in the back pocket of his jeans. Then he takes my left hand in his right hand and squeezes it affectionately.

Is this guy for real?

Sid rolls his eyes and starts to head out the door. As he leaves, I look at the painting again, the mists of color that show how we're a match.

Before he exits through the front door, Sid pokes his head back in. "If I forget to say it later," he says, pointing with a long finger to my canvas, "that one's not terrible."

Not terrible. Perhaps not the most elaborate compliment, but like most things in my life recently, it certainly seems like the start of something promising, if not everything I've always wanted.

*　*　*

Tate and I walk around town after we leave the studios. We look in closed shop windows, eye the freshly poured Oreo fudge at the candy store, and talk about everything from sports pressure to artistic angst. We wind up playing the old board game Chutes and Ladders at the Coffee Dive, the too-small-to-be-called-a-café place that's attached to Downtown Studios. Under the table Tate sandwiches my ankles between his, and on top of the table I kick board game butt. Even though it's a game based on luck and odds, not skill, I feel proud, and he fakes enough wounded pride to look adorable. Then, before we part ways, he kisses me good night.

When I get to my room, the first thing I do is e-mail Alexa all about my evening with Tate. I want to share it with her, even more than I've wanted to share anything with Faye. When I'm typing, I realize that I haven't told Tate yet that Alexa contacted me. It's not as if I'm trying to keep it a secret, but then again, maybe I am.

I guess I just want her all to myself for a while.

FOURTEEN

I don't know everything about Alexa Mason-Cohen; of course I don't. But from the e-mails we've exchanged over the past twenty-four hours, I'm sure she feels she knows me, just the way I feel I know her. We agreed from the beginning that we'd be completely honest with each other, not stopping to edit our thoughts. So far we have exchanged the basics: favorite kind of take-out (both of us *love* Chinese), favorite season (we both like fall but for different reasons—I like the colors, she likes the anticipation of the school year starting), and music tastes (we are going to burn CDs for each other of our favorite songs and explain why each tune is important).

We also agreed not to send jpegs. "I want the first time I see you to be in person," Alexa said in one of her e-mails. I've already learned that it would be hard to argue with this girl, and that's why I haven't. She has asked about fifteen times about making plans to meet each other, and I've only answered back with *?????* because I had a feeling she'd be more than ready to debate me.

Here's the thing that frightens me most: what if I meet her and don't like her? If I keep her at arm's length, maybe I can delay that outcome, or prevent it altogether. If I really let her into my life, I run the risk of either hating her off the bat, which would suck, or liking her so much that it would hurt like hell if I found out something bad about her later or if she didn't end up liking me.

This is what I'm thinking about while I'm lying in bed at two-thirty in the morning. The first chills of fall are creeping into the air and into my room through my half-open window. The breeze makes me pull my covers up to my chin. I think about the great e-mail she sent me in response to my date-with-Tate story.

> *This Tate guy sounds amazing. Into sports AND art AND Chutes and Ladders? I live in Manhattan with millions of boys and I haven't met anyone that well-rounded. You're lucky, Jenny. And even luckier now that you have me! ;-)*

Everything she writes sounds so energetic and sincere. She makes me want to talk even though I don't know what to say. So much so that I script another letter to her in my head. Then I get up, sit down at the computer, and begin typing. Picasso once said that you have to act in painting how you do in life. And maybe that's been part of the reason why my paintings haven't come to life yet.

> *Alexa,*
> *It's way late and I should be asleep, but it's*

still summer so I feel okay about bending rules
and regulations. I hope you can understand,
though, that I'm worried about

Before I can finish it, an e-mail pops up in my inbox. It's from Alexa.

Hey Jenny,
    Enough of this writing thing. Call me when
you get a chance, okay? I wanna know if our
voices are the same! 917 555 3717
            A "Too Excited to Sleep" M-C

I stare at the phone number Alexa sent, and before I'm even aware of reaching for the phone, I dial it. As the ring sounds, I feel calm and happy. All the fear I had before about possibly not liking her has apparently ducked out for a late-night snack or something.

"I can't sleep either," I blurt out to Alexa before she has even said hello.

"Oh my God, we *do* sound alike!" Alexa replies.

I'm sitting on a globular beanbag chair, staring out the window at the night sky as we talk.

"This is so weird," I say.

"Yeah, weird, but very . . ."

"Cool," we say in unison.

Suddenly we are dying of laughter.

I really like how this feels.

After more than an hour goes by, we're still talking about everything under the sun—school, parents, love, and hopes for the future. I'm so comfortable chatting with her that I can't believe I was even stressed out about it before. It reminds me so much of how things happened with Tate.

"So describe yourself in one adjective," Alexa says through a yawn.

"What? That's way too hard." I look out the window and see that the sky is starting to lighten.

"Fine, I'll go first," she laughs. "Impulsive. The way I see it, if you think about something too much before doing it, the chance to do it may be gone by the time you decide. Okay, your turn."

I wince a little. This is the exact opposite of how I see things. Thinking limits the element of surprise. Thinking is what you have to do before you can create. Thinking protects you from making the wrong decision.

"You still there?" Alexa asks.

"Yeah, I'm here." I hear a bird chirping outside, and I want to imagine what it looks like, not go to the window and see for myself. "I'd say that my adjective is thoughtful."

"I should have known," Alexa says.

I have a hunch that she's grinning.

Now the sky resembles the painting I started at the studio. Pinks are merging with oranges. Morning is on the way. We take this as a sign to get some sleep and say our good-byes, but when Alexa's about to hang up, she says, "Wait!"

"What is it?" I rub my eyes and stretch my right arm into the air.

"I think you seem great, and I really think we should meet," she says sweetly.

I draw a deep breath and sigh. Fear has come back and made itself comfortable inside my heart. I wish Tate were here to take this phone out of my grasp and hold my hand. "I think you're cool, too," I reply.

When I crawl back into bed and close my eyes, I hope she isn't too upset that I didn't say anything else.

FIFTEEN

The past two days were a brilliant blur: laughing at Utopia Beach (a place that finally lives up to its name) with Tate, talking on the phone several times with Alexa, swabbing the art decks at Downtown Studios, and avoiding Sid Sleethly so I didn't have to hear his thoughts about my paintings. My pace was faster, my smile wider, my thoughts scattered with the buzz of liking someone who likes me back—and getting to know Alexa.

Every time we talk, I become more and more comfortable thinking of her as my real, true sister, even though I'm aware that Alexa and I share only as many genes as I do with Sierra, Sage, and Russ. Somehow the fact that we found each other in the way we did seems to mean more to me. It's hard to explain.

I've been sitting here with Tate for a few hours, trying to do just that, and he's been patiently listening to me ramble, never interrupting. I'm beginning to think he doesn't have any flaws, even though rationally I know it's impossible. I fiddle with my newly purchased cell phone, then rest it in my lap.

"So, what do you like most about her?" Tate offers a lick of his maple vanilla cone as we lounge on the stone rim of the enoromous fountain in the middle of town. The statue in the center is a child riding a dolphin, the waves splashing but motionless around her. When I was little I used to want to be that girl, riding away to somewhere unknown. But as I look into Tate's gleaming eyes, I know there's no place I'd rather be. I put my phone in my pocket lest I damage another one; then I slide my flip-flops off, spin around, and sit on the edge of the wall so I can dip my feet into the cool water. In the fall the sports teams sometimes come here after big games. Tate has probably dipped his feet in here, or been thrown in, many times. Maybe he's even kissed someone here. I banish the thought.

"This may sound lame, but right now I'm just happy that she exists." I look over my shoulder at Tate and use my hand as a visor. The sun is shining so hard. "When I talk to her, I feel as though I have a tether out there. A mooring in—"

"In the ocean of the world?" Tate interrupts me for the first time with his sarcasm.

"Joke all you want, Bro, but it's true."

Tate crunches the last of his cone and spins around so he's facing the water alongside me. "Fitz, don't call me Bro."

My brow furrows at this unexpected announcement. "Why not?"

Tate shrugs and looks off in the distance. Every once in a while I wonder if he's thinking about what's ahead for us. Do I fit somewhere in the equation that adds the sports season to the back-to-school season? I really hope I do. He takes my hand, brings it up to his mouth, and lightly presses his lips to my palm. "I'm Bro when I'm with the team. When I'm with you, I'd rather be Tate."

I know exactly what he means.

He tucks a lock of my hair behind my ear and goes in for a kiss when my cell phone rings. He smiles. "Let me guess? The great Alexa is on the line. I'll take off."

I look at the phone. He's right; it's her. I really want to pick up, but I don't want him to go, either. "Stay. I'll only be a minute."

Tate has that faraway look on his face again. "It's fine. You should take your time talking to her. I have to run sprints, anyway. The first game is around the corner."

When he walks away and I think about how soon we will be forced back to our old worlds, I make a wish that summer could last forever.

"It's like I can feel August being sucked down the drain." I'm wandering through the town square, cutting across the green so I'm near Downtown Studios. On the way I count twelve signs for the art show, and with each glance at them, I feel another level of anxiety: I have to get into that show, otherwise I have to wait a whole year before trying for it again. And by then who knows what will have happened or where I will be?

"I know what you mean," Alexa reassures. "The city's practically deserted. My moms usually rent this house in the Hamptons for the last couple weeks of August, but they didn't this year."

Alexa's two mothers are both lawyers who seem eternally busy, always dashing in for late meals and leaving at the crack of dawn. At least, that's how she tells it.

"Did you finish any paintings for the show?" she asks. "There's not much time, you know. Maybe you should just pull an all-nighter and drink lots of Red Bull and just whip something up. That's what what I would do."

"Thanks for putting the pressure on," I say, and smile. "Art's not like that. You have to think a lot about what you're trying to create. At least, I do. Besides, I can't stand the taste of Red Bull. I'm more of a root beer float kind of person."

Alexa laughs, and I like the sound of it. Her laugh can best be described as a cross between a sneeze and a giggle. "Well, start thinking hard, Jenny. You only have another week."

I can't stop grinning. It's actually *nice* to have someone care enough about my painting to be on my back about it. My parents have known me all my life and they've never shown as much interest as Alexa is now. "I still have a few more days before Sid makes his final decisions, and I promise to work hard. What about you? When do you leave for the beach?"

I hear street noise in the background: bus brakes squealing, people honking. "I'm checking on my project," Alexa says. "It's really loud here, but it'll get better once the trees grow."

For some reason I thought Alexa would be an artist, too, but she's not. (Maybe I've seen too many Disney movies about twins separated at birth.) In fact, she single-handedly coordinated a coalition at school to raise funding to turn a local run-down former tire factory into a children's center with a huge outdoor park. It was an impulse of hers after reading about the plight of the urban child in the *New York Times*.

"Hold on, I have to move something," Alexa says. She grunts into the phone and then comes back. "Sorry. There are still a lot of finishing touches to make. Paint the fence, plant the last of the shrubs. But it's going to be great!"

"I wish I could see it," I say.

"You *can* see it. All you have to do is get your butt on a train!" The excitement in her voice ripples through the phone wires.

I bite my lip. My instinct tells me that I need more time to prepare and think about how a visit might go. But when I stop and really check my feelings, I know it's not an instinct—it's fear. Fear that if I go there, it might be too hard to leave her behind.

"Jenny, just come in for the weekend. It'll be fun!" I don't want to push her away again, but that's what I end up doing. "I can't," I say. "Like you said, I have to focus on my painting."

I feel so bad for turning her words against her. Why am I doing this?

"I did say that, you're right."

Her voice is thin and shallow, not upbeat and enthusiastic as before. I look up at the clear blue sky, noticing the darkest leaves on the trees and thinking about how soon they will morph into reds and oranges. I have to level with her. "The thing is, and please don't take this the wrong way . . ." Beads of sweat form on my upper lip.

Silence from Alexa. All I can hear is more street noise. And then she speaks. "You haven't told your family yet, have you?"

I look down at my feet in shame. "No."

"My moms were in this right from the beginning," she says. "Your parents will be so supportive."

I shake my head. "You don't even know them. They're not like that."

"Maybe you need to give them a chance." She waits for me to say something, but I can't. All I can picture is how awkward it would be to face them. Won't they assume that I went to find Alexa because something was wrong with our family dynamic? It's kind of true, but it's one thing for them to suspect it, and another thing for them to know it for sure.

Alexa clears her throat. "Jenny? You still there?"

"Yeah."

"Listen, if you can't come to see me because you have to work, I could come visit you."

In the middle of the busy summer street, where Popsicles drip down kids' arms, where parents chase their toddlers, where people on their lunch breaks sit on the benches eating sandwiches, I feel everything stop. Alexa Mason-Cohen could come here and meet my world. And then the biggest fear of all hits me.

What if she doesn't like me?

My heart is racing so fast I can barely answer her. "I'm not sure."

"Well, guess what?" she says confidently. "I am sure enough for the both of us. Take that!"

All of a sudden I'm laughing so hard I grip my side.

"Okay, okay, you've worn me down." I must give in to the unknown this time. Tate, I'm sure, would agree. "How about the day after tomorrow? I can break the news to my parents and clean up and everything."

"Oh, you don't have to clean, Jenny. I'm family, remember?" She says this with such conviction that I almost look forward to telling my parents.

Almost.

SIXTEEN

"Will you pass the butter?" I ask, wishing that somehow my mom would interpret this phrase as *I have a half sister, and her name is Alexa.*

"Sure, honey," my mom says, handing me the cow-shaped butter dish. "Anything else?"

Alexa's coming to visit. I think you'll really like her!

"No, this is great. Thanks." I spread a pat of butter onto my steaming ear of corn. When I gaze out the kitchen window, I see that the patio is slick with fresh rain. The showers hit suddenly, as soon as I got home with the twins. It was as if Mother Nature knew I was about to blow the lid off our normal family routine.

It's such a typical scene, the kind of dinner that screams the words *everyday, normal, plain.* I survey the cast of characters and the setting, and bottle up the tension and excitement about what the day after tomorrow will bring. Namely, another person at this table. Another person, who shares my genes and no one else's here. If I only knew how to tell everyone.

I watch my dad as he eats his corn. He's like an old-fashioned typewriter, sliding the cob back and forth, only eating one row at a time. He juts his lower teeth forward and chomps down hard, sending a few bits of corn flying into the air.

"Daaad!" Sierra whines, wiping a piece of stray corn from her T-shirt. "Stop being so gross!"

"Sorry," he says with a grin. He holds up the cob with the neat rows of pecked corn. "My technique may not be the most delicate, but it works."

I pick up the ear from my plate, holding it by the ends. It's hot, so I drop it quickly. My mom flits to the other side of the table, opening the drawer at the end of it and handing me two plastic corn holders in the shape of hot dogs.

"Here," she says. "You don't want to get burned."

"Mom, I'm fine. I can hold it without those things." I pluck them off the ends of my ear, where she's shoved them in. "Plus, it freaks me out that they're hot dogs. What does that have to do with corn?"

Everyone at the table laughs. "That's a good point," my mother says.

"Maybe they're just supposed to symbolize picnics?" I suggest.

"Maybe. But what I want to know, Jenny, is how do you eat your corn?" Dad says in a playful tone.

"Uh-oh," Russ says. "Is this one of those psychological games that reveal something about you?"

Dad bites his corn again. "It's more of a theory that I'm tinkering with. For instance, look at Sage and Sierra. They take a bite, chew it, and then turn the ear of corn in a circle, making rings."

The twins look at their ears of corn and their nearly identical patterns of marks.

Dad continues, "Then we've got you, Russ. You're all over the place."

We all chuckle when Russ shows us his ear of corn. "It's pretty hacked up," he says, pointing out the patches gnawed down to the cob.

I actually kind of like this game. It's about observation and paying attention to detail—two things that any good artist needs to do.

"Well, Mom's big into the bite 'n' slide routine," I say, pointing to the corn on her plate. "She takes a careful bite and then goes to the exact same spot side to side, whereas Dad works row to row."

Dad smiles at me proudly. He hasn't done this in ages. "Good job, Jenny. So what do you think? Are you more like Mom, or are you more like me?"

Suddenly, I'm blinking back tears while staring at the butter melting on my plate. Slick and colorless, it reminds me of diluted paint. It doesn't even occur to my dad that I might have my own unique style of corn eating, like the twins or Russ. And yet when I think about what makes me different from all of them, I wish I could be up in my closet, alone and safe with my canvases.

But I have to tell them about Alexa, and I have to tell them now. I'm sure they can see that something's wrong, anyway.

Sierra picks at her plate nervously. Perhaps for once she can sense how I'm feeling. "Jenny, I've got something important to tell you," she says, her voice quivering.

Oh, the irony, I think as I spear a leaf of lettuce with my salad fork. "Out with it, Sierra."

She glances at Sage and then swallows hard. "Our recital is on September fifth."

September fifth is the day of the art show. I think I've said this out loud, but no one is reacting, so maybe I haven't. Not that it matters—Sierra and Sage have obviously seen the signs around town and made the connection on their own. I take my fork and begin stabbing at the piece of chicken on my plate because I know that in a head-to-head matchup with the twins, I always lose. I feel defeated right now, to the point where I can't even begin to think about revealing my secret, which I told both Alexa and Tate I'd do. All I can see is red, and I snap.

"Why haven't you visited me at Downtown Studios, Dad? I've been there working hard all summer, and you haven't made the trip. It's as if the building were located on top of a mountain or something." My tone is sharp and bitter. I don't like the sound of it, but I can't help it, either. "You and Mom always seem to make time for Sierra and Sage's special event of the moment."

My dad leans back in his chair, looking confused.

"You also managed to attend Russ's tryouts for all-state in the middle of mediating the Wilson case, which you said was the toughest you've ever had to contend with. They were *tryouts*! Not even the real thing."

"They still count," Russ says, slightly dejected.

"Jenny . . ." My mom is using her *settle down* voice.

I push myself away from the table and stand up. "You don't get it, do you? I'm so sick of being treated like the reject Fitzgerald."

Dad wipes his mouth with his napkin and tosses it on the table. He appears annoyed. "No one feels that way, Jen."

"Well, guess what? *I* feel that way!" I'm shouting now. This isn't going to help matters, but I still keep pressing. "Dad, you didn't answer me. Why haven't you made the effort to come and see my work?"

Mom shakes her head as she begins to clear the table. Sierra and Sage are silent for once, stacking the dishes into piles. Russ wolfs down another roll while he listens.

"Sometimes, Jenny, it's as though you can't see what's right in front of you," Dad says with a sigh.

"What's that supposed to mean?"

Sierra and Sage whisper something and my mother shoots them a look. Russ shrugs at me helplessly.

"You haven't asked us to come, Jenny. Not once," my dad says simply.

I put my hands on my hips and look down at my sneakers. I'm suddenly aware of why I'm so fixated on arguing with him—it's a distraction from the conversation that we really need to have. Besides, it's true. I never asked anyone to come see me at work in the studio. Even Tate invited himself along the other night.

"We don't want to rush you," my mom says. The water from the sink is making a waterfall sound in the stainless steel basin, reminding me of that beautiful fountain in town. I wish I were on the stone dolphin now, being carried away to somewhere else. "We just thought that when you were ready to have us there, you'd let us know."

The doorbell rings, and it barely registers on my radar. I'm too caught up in my emotions to care who's on the front porch. "Well then, I'll be ready on September fifth, the day of the art show."

Mom and Dad exchange surprised glances. They know they're going to have to make a choice here. I study Dad as he thinks of what to say. He's always careful with his words; because of his line of work, he knows how powerful they can be. However, when I take notice of how long the big gaping pause is, and how hard he has to think about this, I don't give him the chance to say anything.

"Forget it. I was crazy to expect you and Mom to duck out on the twins' precious Dance Project performance."

"Ours is more important," Sage says, and we all turn to look at her. Sierra's mouth hangs open. Even she didn't see that coming, or maybe she thought the same thing but had the sense to keep it to herself.

"Sage! That's a terrible thing to say," my mom scolds.

"Well, I'm sorry, it *is*," Sage pleads. "Jenny can paint whatever anytime and show it to you guys. We have this huge deal on *one day*."

I never noticed the resemblance between Sage and Sid Sleethly until now. Just as I did when Tate was with me in the studio, I wonder if Alexa Mason-Cohen would defend me if she were here. I find a source of strength from inside me when I remind myself that I'll find out the day after tomorrow. I'll know so much more then, and perhaps feel so much better.

"You know what? It doesn't matter. If I get accepted into

the art show, I don't need you there. Go see the twins. I'll be fine." My words are firm and confident, not mean and sour like before. Alexa is not even here yet, and she's somehow already helping me.

"Hey guys, look who's here," Russ says from behind me.

I turn around and see Tate standing by his side. "Hi, Jenny," he says.

"Hey, you." I'm sure my big smile is a dead giveaway to everyone in the room.

Russ sprints over to the table and chucks Tate a dinner roll. "You guys can let us finish cleaning up in here."

But my dad still wants to finish our discussion. "I want to support you, Jenny. We all do."

He's about to say more, but Tate doesn't realize this, which is probably why he excitedly interrupts. "So everything's cool, then?"

"What do you mean, Bro?" Russ crumples up a napkin and lobs it into the wastebasket.

"You know, Jenny's big announcement!" Tate says. "About Alexa?"

I almost faint when these words escape Tate's luscious lips.

"Who's Alexa?" my dad asks.

"Yeah, who is Alexa?" Sierra repeats.

"You didn't tell them? Oh, Fitz, I'm so sorry." Tate runs his hands through his hair, looking as though he wishes he could curl up into a ball and be hiked out into a field somewhere. He just unknowingly stole an important moment from me, but I'm not mad at him for it. I'm practically grateful. Now I can't avoid it any longer.

"What's going on?" Mom's eyebrows rise with curiosity as she dries her hands on a dish towel.

When I don't answer her, everyone stands motionless and stares at me.

"Jenny, who is Alexa?" Dad asks again. The worry in his voice is echoing the looks on my family's faces.

I clutch my hands together behind my back, wringing them the way I do after I paint for too long and they ache. Only now I'm aching on the inside, and the only way to make it go away is to let everything out.

"Alexa is my half sister, and she's coming here soon. Really soon."

SEVENTEEN

Shock doesn't adequately describe the look on my dad's face when my statement finally sinks in. Tate hangs way back in the corner of the kitchen and leans against the stool that usually acts as our mail table.

"I don't understand," Dad says for the fifth time. I've explained everything to him already—how I read the article; how I found Alexa through the Web site; and how after talking on the phone a bunch of times, she wanted to meet me—but none of it is making sense to him. Dad is pacing back and forth, shaking his head. "Why? Why would you want to go looking?"

"She didn't do it because there's anything lacking here." Mom is sitting down at the kitchen table, trying to remain calm. She tilts her head at me. "Did you?"

I'm stationed near the refrigerator, pulling at a stray thread at the bottom of my hooded sweatshirt. "No, not really." The strained look on my face is a dead giveaway, too. "Dad, if you thought you had a brother or a sister out in the world somewhere, wouldn't you want to know?"

"Half brother or sister, you mean," Dad says sharply.

"Hey, Russ and the twins are my half siblings, too," I say. "Half is all I've got."

For someone who is so good at settling other people's problems, my father is pretty resistant to the unexpected, and to change. But maybe we all are. I sneak a look at Tate. I can tell he feels guilty for all this.

Sierra finally speaks up. "Are we not, like, enough sister for you?" She doesn't resemble Sid anymore. She resembles a drooping flower that was rained on too much.

Now I'm feeling guilty. I don't think I was fully aware of how much this might affect everyone else. Does that make me selfish? "It's not that at all. I just wanted to see if there was someone out there who had more in common with me."

"Well, you should've asked permission," Dad grunts. "And how do you know that this isn't some sort of scam?"

"A scam?" My eyebrows are raised to the point of distorting my face. I'm trying to paint a picture of what my dad looked like when I was a child, but my canvas is blank. "Well, you can call her moms if you want."

"Her *moms*?" Dad's voice raises about twelve octaves. "Jenny, do you have any idea what you're getting yourself into? Have you even thought this through?"

"Calm down, honey," Mom says to Dad. The rest of my family and Tate slink out into the living room, where they'll hear everything we say but not be right in the center of the storm.

"Jenny?" Mom touches my shoulder and I flinch, thinking she's going to scold me.

"What'd I do wrong now?" I try not to sound bitter, but I am. Why can't they just be excited for me?

"It's not that you did anything wrong," Mom says.

My dad rolls his eyes. "Yes, she did."

Mom throws him a stern look and then turns back to me. "You have every right to seek out someone who may be connected to you. However, we never hid how you were conceived, Jenny, and you shouldn't have hid this from us."

"Well, if I didn't have to worry about your reaction, maybe I wouldn't have."

"Fair enough," my mom says reasonably.

But my dad is definitely not in a reasonable mood. "Even so, I don't think it's a good idea for *her* to visit."

I square off against him. "You can say *her* name. A-lex-a."

"Drop the tone, Jennifer," Mom barks. She's going to side with him. They are unified, a team. "Alexa's visit can wait until we've all had a chance to discuss the implications of this."

I can't believe what I'm hearing, and at the same time, I knew they would say exactly this. "Why won't you guys trust me on this one?"

"Why should we trust you when you did this behind our backs?" Dad's voice raises to sonic level.

I stomp my feet on the floor like a little kid. This is what he's reduced me to. "Well, I already invited her."

He doesn't scream or yell this, he just says it flatly, without any feeling at all: "I guess you'll have to *un*invite her."

I am willing myself not to cry. "Don't I have a say in this?"

Dad crosses his arms over his chest. He's said before that

this is body language meant to convey the end of a conversation.

Mom gets up from the table and stands by his side. "We're not saying you can't see her ever, Jenny. Just not now. We need some time."

The gentle way she says this makes me feel hopeful. Maybe all this drama will blow over soon.

And then Dad puts the last nail in the coffin. "Jenny, I want you to go upstairs and call her to cancel the visit *now*."

His words suck the hope right out of me, and he storms out of the room before I can say anything more.

EIGHTEEN

Last night didn't go as planned.

I went upstairs as my father ordered me to, and I even picked up the phone to call Alexa, but I couldn't bring myself to dial. The thought of hearing disappointment in her voice kept me up half the night, too. When I woke up this morning, I decided that I would e-mail her—sure, it's the easy way out, but it's better than nothing. I'll do it after breakfast. That way, I can think of all the right things to say.

Who am I kidding?

I'm halfway down the stairs when the doorbell rings. The only person awake this early and on the neighborhood prowl is the FedEx guy. But when I open the door, I find someone else instead.

"Tate!" The exuberance in my voice takes even me by surprise. He looks like he just rolled out of bed. His hair is sticking up in the back, and he's wearing this pair of gray sweatpants with a small hole in the knee. I wrap my arms around him and he hugs me tightly.

"Can we talk?" he whispers in my ear.

I pull away a bit so I can look into his eyes. There's a lash on his right cheek, and I wipe it away with my thumb. "Sure. I have a few minutes."

"A lot can happen in a few minutes," he says before sweetly kissing me on the mouth.

We walk over to the unlandscaped area in the backyard. Tate wedges his legs between six ten-pound bags of gravel. The bags are stacked, slumped one on the next, creating a column of space in between the sacks. Near the bags are unearthed plants and shrubs, and an uneven pile of stone bricks my dad envisions being neatly aligned one day.

"There's room for two," Tate says. The space is just large enough for us both to fit comfortably and remain unseen by anyone else, closed off by the garden supplies.

"So, what's up?" I ask while taking one of his hands in mine.

"I came by to say I'm sorry for getting you into trouble." Tate kicks his soles onto the brown gravel bags, but they don't shift. "I should have minded my own business."

I can feel the calluses on Tate's hand with my fingers. Years of football have toughened them up. "It's okay. They would have reacted like that if I had told them to begin with."

Tate kisses me on the cheek. "So we're okay?"

"Of course we're okay."

He looks down at the ground. "Did I ever tell you that my mom is an art dealer?"

My eyes widen. "No, you didn't."

"Yeah. When other kids were reading *Goodnight Moon*, my mom would show me those huge art books. Anyway, there's this painting, by Mondrian."

"*Broadway Boogie Woogie?*" I ask. I can see the colors so clearly in my mind it's as though the canvas is next to us.

Tate smiles and shifts his weight a little so we can look at one another without neck strain. "I love that painting. All the reds and yellows are intersecting like city streets. Everything bounces—the colors, the angles. You almost feel as though you're in motion, just by looking at it." He clears his throat nervously. "That's how I feel when I'm with you."

"You do?" My heart is fluttering so fast that my breathing becomes shallow.

"Yeah. You know, the other day I didn't come over here to see Russ about sports stuff. I just needed an excuse to see you."

I put my arm around his waist, and he tucks me under his shoulder. "Well, now you don't need an excuse."

"Good," he says, playfully touching my nose with the tip of his finger. "Speaking of which, do you have a good excuse for not calling her last night?"

Now I definitely can't breathe. "How did you know I didn't call her?"

Tate grins. "You can't fool me, Fitz."

I am amazed by this guy. Completely, totally amazed.

"Come here," he says. We kiss again, and I inhale the smell of him—a blend of spices and citrus and sleep. It makes me want to dig into the tubes of paint I've never used, the bruise-dark eggplant color and the hefty cream, and mix them and see what happens.

He pulls away a little and leans his head against mine. "I can't believe school starts in a few days."

In one moment summer slips away and we're back in the

corridor with the crush of cliques and other obstacles that may end up coming between us. "I know."

I wait for him to say something else, something that will reassure me that things will stay this way when autumn is in full swing, but he doesn't. I put my arms around him, and we stand there, hugging and then kissing until I realize that time is fleeting and there's something I can't put off any longer.

"Tate, I have to go." I squeeze Tate's hands and he squeezes mine back. We leave our little hideaway, and he walks me back to the front door.

"I know you're not one for sports pep talks, Fitz," he says with a grin. "But my coach told me once that preparing for the unexpected doesn't do anyone any good. It only takes your mind away from the experience."

When he kisses me and dashes off into the morning breeze, I know without a doubt or a shred of fear that experience is what life's all about.

A few minutes later I'm sitting in my closet, surrounded by paints, holding my phone in my hand. I decided as I climbed up the stairs that I wasn't going to take the easy e-mail way out. I'm about ready to dial when Russ pokes his head in.

"Hey, Jen?"

My eyes are fixed on the phone. "Yeah?"

"What's she like?" he asks. Russ was notably silent during the sister-inquisition downstairs last night. I wonder what he's thinking.

"Impulsive." I smile as I say this, remembering our first conversation and how surreal it was. "Honestly, Russ, I guess I don't know what she's like. Not really. I mean, how can you truly know anything without spending time with someone?"

Russ kneels down in front of me, so I have no choice but to look up at him. "She's not just *someone*," he says, searching my face for a clue about how to deal with all this.

But I don't have one.

My mother yells up the stairs for Russ to answer the door. He still rests his eyes on mine. "Jenny, sometimes, with sisters, you don't have to know *everything* to know everything."

Then he pats me on the shoulder and darts out of my room.

I dial Alexa's number with Russ's words lingering in my mind. My ear is pressed so hard to the phone it will probably leave a red mark. I still don't know what to say.

Outside, I hear the crunch of gravel on the driveway. My dad is probably getting ready to go to work, precooling his car so it's icy when he gets in. There are two rings and then I hear her.

"Hey!" Alexa's voice is chirpy.

"Hey," I reply in a dark tone that foreshadows the bad news to come. I want to get straight to the point. "Alexa, I'm really sorry to have to tell you this, but—"

She cuts me off excitedly. "Whatever bummer you're about to unload, just wait."

"No, Alexa, listen to me—"

"Jenny, shut up for a sec." Her grin is nearly audible.

From downstairs Russ shouts, "Jen!"

And then, as if there weren't enough chaos, my dad beeps from the driveway. Suddenly I remember I didn't close the windows on my car. It's one of Dad's big pet peeves. I can just hear him now: "What if it rained and your seats got wet? What if someone stole the radio?" Never mind that it was clear last night and the radio isn't worth borrowing, let alone stealing.

"Jenny!" my mother yells from the bottom of the stairs.

"Hang on, Alexa." I keep the phone to my ear and walk to the top of the stairs to deal with whatever frenzy is happening.

My mother has one hand on her hip and the other over her mouth as though she's just tasted something very spicy. The twins, all set for camp, are backed up to the wall with their eyebrows raised. Russ looks up at me helplessly.

"What's wrong?" I ask, covering the phone with my hand.

Russ points to the window that looks out onto the front porch, which I can't see from the top stair. Slowly, I make my way to the window. Outside on the gravel, my dad is staring at something at the end of the driveway. When I look in the same direction, I see a girl standing in front of a red taxi, holding a cell phone.

I swallow hard and then my hands start shaking. "Alexa?" I say into the phone.

The girl in the driveway looks at me and nods. "Here I am!"

NINETEEN

Once I'm on the stoop, I'm hit by the sheer force of seeing Alexa for the first time, and by the stony look on my dad's face. Alexa drops her oversized black bag on the ground and throws her arms around me in a big embrace. I hug her back, still shaking, while Dad continues to glare at me from his position on the uneven gravel.

"Can you believe it?" Alexa's eyes are everywhere—looking at me, taking in the house, and pausing on each one of my family members as they emerge from the doorway.

"It—it's a . . . ," I stutter, wondering what to say. "I didn't . . ."

Dad clears his throat, sidestepping Alexa and coming straight at me. "Was I unclear last night?" He's seething as he leans down to talk to me. Alexa stands there, her mouth twisted in a knot of confusion.

I can feel everything around me—the stones poking through the thin rubber of my drugstore flip-flops, the hot air prickling up my back, the stares from my siblings as they watch this unfold. "Dad, I—"

"You deliberately disobeyed me," he says, anger spilling from his mouth into the air.

I feel like a dog who went astray, and my own anger roils inside. "I was going to! I tried—"

Alexa steps forward to say something but my dad turns his back to her and touches my shoulder. "You *tried*? You don't *attempt* to make a phone call. You just do it. Really, Jenny, I'm disappointed in you." He storms off without an introduction to Alexa, and I'm left to pick up the pieces of her surprise visit.

My mother says hello, nicely but not in the most overjoyed way, and the twins tentatively shake her hand. Russ gives her his standard wave and a "hey" and then it's just the two of us. Me and Alexa. Alone together.

When we get upstairs and settle in my room, Alexa's words zoom out fast. "I was all set to come tomorrow, you know? Like we planned. Then I just got this feeling that I had to jump on a train, right now. So I shoved my stuff in here." She kicks her black bag. "I don't know. Maybe I was worried that you were going to chicken out."

"Chicken out? It's not a drag race," I say, joking. My mind is speeding, like when I wake from a dream and have a great idea for a painting, only I can't grasp exactly what it was. I wonder if I should demand that Dad hear me out while I explain that I didn't deliberately go against him. How was I to suspect Alexa would show up without notice? It's not anything I'd ever do, so it never dawned on me.

"I can't believe you're here," I say as I nervously twist my watch around and around on my wrist. The whole time

I was outside with Tate this morning, she was already on her way here. While I was eating my cereal, she was watching the scenery slide by, each blur of green bringing her closer to me. The only way I could have stopped her was to have called her right away after Dad asked. But given how impulsive Alexa is, would that have even worked?

"You really don't like surprises, do you?" She turns to me and we just stare at one another for a long time, letting the visuals sink in. Alexa grins as she tilts her head. She has long straight hair the color of the inside of corn, and it's parted to the right side. No matter what I do, my hair automatically parts itself down the middle.

"Not really." This is the understatement of the year. But I can't exactly say I loathe being shocked when she's just shown up a day early. I also feel the urge to groan about how much trouble she's gotten me into, but instead I focus my attention on Alexa's magenta Indian print top. "I like that color. I use it to paint."

"I'd love to see some of your work," she says. And then when I flinch, she adds, "When you're ready."

"You have much thicker hair than I thought," I say, and realize it sounds a little strange. Then again, the whole thing is strange.

"That's funny," Alexa says, looking at me from my shoes all the way to my ears. "Do you do that a lot?"

"What?" I can't believe I'm standing here in my bedroom, having a face-to-face conversation with her.

"Picture how things should be before they actually happen?" Alexa says offhandedly.

"Sort of, I guess."

In my life drawing class last year, I learned how to approximate muscle tone on the paper or canvas. It's useful, but not as much as getting a feeling for what's in front of you. I take a deep breath. The sunlight through the window hits Alexa's back, giving her an outline that glows. That's what I'd draw right now. Her semihalo.

"I'm so not like that," Alexa says. She sounds proud of this, like it's the way to be. "It's a waste of time."

Suddenly I feel as if I'm being criticized. I don't reply, but that doesn't stop Alexa from saying more.

"If you live in your head too much, it can take the place of the real thing." Alexa takes off the magenta top to reveal a tight tank top underneath, which highlights her athletic build.

"Well, my dad doesn't like surprises, either," I say, marveling at the fact that I just pointed out a similarity between him and me.

Alexa shrugs. Her body language is definitely more animated than mine. I hadn't thought that I'd notice our differences this much. "Good to know," she says, and smiles.

When I close the bedroom door behind us, I wonder how much there is for us to know, and if most of it will be good.

TWENTY

After a long afternoon of hanging out in my room and trading stories, I take Alexa with me to pick up the twins from camp. I put art supplies in and slam the trunk of the car shut, and Alexa slides into the passenger seat. She puts one hand on the roof as she gets in, just like I do.

I tell myself I'm not going to do a constant running tab of what's the same and what's not, but it's hard not to. Alexa lifts her hair off her back and ties it in a knot that stays put without an elastic. My hair could never do this in a million years.

"Jenny," she says when I start the car. "I am so psyched to be here."

I have my hands on the steering wheel and my eyes on the rearview mirror as I back out of the driveway, but I nod to her. "Me too."

"It's like, I have a whole other family here that I'm getting to know. And you have one waiting for you in New York."

If only it were that simple. There is a string of complications that Alexa somehow doesn't seem to see.

"The truth is," I say to her when I put on my turn signal, "dealing with Team Fitz isn't going to be easy." I look at her before pulling onto the road. "Don't expect a giant welcome dinner, is all I'm saying." Alexa nods, taking in the info but not looking damaged by it. If I were in her position, I'd want to back down, hop on the next train home, and start all over.

"Plus, there's my painting. I have so little time." I say this while Alexa fiddles with her tank top, smoothing out the straps on her tanned shoulders. I'm in the middle of stressing about getting the artwork done, and imagining the massive tension that will invade my house once Dad comes home, when I hear a car horn sound behind me. I'm driving all of ten miles per hour. Yikes.

"You think too much, Jenny." Alexa leans forward and fiddles with the radio. "We have the same fingers, by the way. Do you see?" she asks, holding out her hands.

I nod. "Yeah. Your middle finger is almost the same exact length of your ring finger, like mine."

"And our thumbs are exactly alike." Alexa smiles with satisfaction as she looks out the window. We drive through the camp gates, and she peers out the open window, her hair flying in the breeze.

"Our thumbs." It's a small thing, just a tiny overlap, but it feels good.

A few minutes later Sierra and Sage leap into the car with a flurry of tights and legs, costumes and flailing hands that demonstrate just how revved up they are about the dance performance. They don't say hello to either of us and immediately begin to gush.

"They said we're good!" Sage exclaims. "We're in the front for at least half of the show."

"Well, I can't wait to see it!" This is the first thing Alexa says to them when she turns around on her knees to make eye contact. When I twist my head and look into the back of the car, I see that the twins have their solidarity pose on—their arms are crossed in front of their chests defensively. But Alexa doesn't see this complication and doesn't back off. She just serves up compliments instead. "I'm sure you both have great form. It's obvious you're built for dancing. Anyone can see that."

They don't budge, and keep silent. I shrug and Alexa gives me a knowing glance. With the twins in the back and me and Alexa up front, it's the first time I feel well-matched, ready to take on whatever my family flings my way.

"You guys don't look alike," Sage says, looking from me to Alexa and back as though we're a tennis match. The tone in her voice suggests that she wants to chip away at me.

"It's not like we're twins." I stare at their faces in the rearview mirror, wishing for a second that Alexa and I did have identical genes; that she'd shown up wearing exactly what I've got on, with some dried paint on her thigh or a consummate knowledge of visual art. Something that would prove how connected we are.

"Jenny and I have the same eyes. I'll show you when we get home," Alexa says.

I can't help but notice Alexa has referred to our house as

133

home. However, what I notice even more is that the twins don't speak at all for the rest of the ride.

"Just so you know," I whisper to Alexa as I pull into the driveway after a fifteen-minute trek through suburbia, "their dance performance is on the same night as the art show."

When I park in front of the house, I wonder if Alexa cares as much as I do that the last days of summer are trickling away. Then again, she doesn't have to worry about spending her afternoons trying to paint and avoid as many Fitz family outings as possible. She doesn't have to think about the carnival and the art show and Tate.

"Ew, that sucks." Alexa seems to take in every detail of the driveway, the exterior of the house, the lawn.

"Yeah. But you'll come to the art show, right?" I make it a question even though I'm sure I know the answer. If the goal is to spend as much time together as possible before she goes back to her posh private school in the city, then Alexa will surely be there.

"I'll have to see. I don't actually know how long I'll be staying."

"Oh." My heart completely deflates, and then my father's appearance in the yard makes my heart stop. He looks every bit as angry and cold as before. The engine noise quiets, the twins sprint out of the car and rush inside, and Alexa and I leave the bubble of the car and head into the flush of family life, as sisters.

* * *

It's make-your-own-rice-bowl night at the Fitzgerald house, and we're in a line, à la all-you-can-eat buffet. Containers of rice, peas, roasted carrots cut on the diagonal, sautéed spinach, baked beans, strips of teriyaki chicken, and steamed broccoli are set on the counter. In a row, my family doesn't seem too intimidating. Maybe it's because like this, shuffling from one food station to the next, it's like the school cafeteria. Sure, it can suck sometimes with dropped trays and with social circles ostracizing and enveloping you, but it's over after a few minutes and you can retreat to the safety of your next class. Only here the safety would be in my room, alone with Alexa.

"Teams, by definition, imply a bond that's unnatural," Alexa says, continuing a conversation she and Russ started while setting the table. I know from experience that this comment of hers will raise my dad's blood pressure. Teams are sacred to him. The church of baseball, the temple of tennis—a look of serenity and peace washes over him when he sees games played; when he's a part of them; or even when the implements of bat, ball, or net are nearby. This is how I feel about tubes of paint, brushes, and palettes—the calm and thrill of walking into an art supply store. But somehow no one else in my family can see that.

"Teams are sacred," Dad says, voicing his opinion firmly. I want to squeeze his hand and tell him I knew he'd say that, but he's at one end of the line, hurling broccoli florets into his oversized green bowl. He tosses the vegetables in a little too forcefully, a sure sign that Alexa's presence is getting to him.

Mom tries to make up for Dad's semi-cold shoulder.

"Maybe there's another side to this, though." She's not overtly defending Alexa—God forbid—but trying to placate us. "Teams can make you feel—"

"Excluded." The word slips out of my mouth and I can't take it back. I imagine we are all shapes, jutting angles over each other, pointing and circling the connections. What are the teams here? The twins versus me and Russ, or me and Alexa versus the rest of my siblings? Parents against kids? Me and Alexa versus everyone else?

Alexa mixes beans into her bowl, clutches a pair of chopsticks, and heads to the table, where she wedges herself in next to Sage, where Sierra always sits. I wait for the fallout. Sierra comes to the table and stops in her tracks when she sees her chair occupied by Alexa. But before Sierra can protest, Alexa intervenes, waving to her enthusiastically.

"Come, sit!" Alexa pats the seat on her other side so she's flanked by my sisters. I'm caught between feeling glad she stuck up for herself (even with a little thing like where to sit) and annoyed because it feels like one step away from me. Alexa keeps feeding the tense conversation. "It's not that I don't like teams. I do!"

Dad turns his icy gaze to Alexa. He can scare anyone with just a look. "Really? Do you play on any?"

It's obvious he expects her to say she doesn't. Then Dad will feel her argument is weak. It happened to me when I tried to dispute the camaraderie he claims is "natural" when you play sports. Not, in my opinion, if you can't play them.

Alexa nods, her confidence steady while Dad cross-examines her. She chews her mouthful of rice and swallows, then explains. "I play on a couple of teams at the varsity level." She sips her water. I notice my father's eyebrows peak as he absorbs this information. My own brows are raised, too. I assumed that Alexa would be—if not dressed completely in black and an art maven—missing the athletic gene, too. Another step away from Team Jen and Alexa and toward the other side. I shouldn't see it like that, but I do. "I also do modern dance with Marissa Lillian," she adds.

An audible gasp from Sierra and Sage. They lean forward so they can look at each other over Alexa, their mouths agape. "Marissa Lillian?" Sage says in disbelief. "She's, like—"

"The most famous dancer ever." Sierra continues the sentence, making me wonder if Alexa and I will ever complete one another's thoughts.

"Yeah, I'm into a lot of activities," Alexa dots her mouth with her napkin. She doesn't seem boastful, just self-assured, as if studying with this world-renowned dancer's troupe is normal.

"That's the coolest thing ever," Sage says, her eyes wide with awe. A pang of jealousy flits into my body, stinging my skin. I rub my arms and push my plate away.

My mother watches me during the whole dinner, and though she joins in the conversation, I can tell that part of her is somewhere else. Maybe she wishes she hadn't told me about my conception, or maybe she hopes all this will blow over, Alexa will leave, and this shift in family dynamics will end as suddenly as it began. But family—genetic or otherwise—isn't like that.

Dad bumps into me when he clears his plate, his body tense and unwavering.

I decide to appeal to him. "Dad, I didn't ask her to come, you know." I bring my dish up to the sink.

He scrubs the rice pot hard and doesn't look at me. "Oh, so she just appeared here as if by magic?"

"Dad," I plead, trying to catch his gaze. Alexa watches me from the table. I don't want her to think I'm turning against her, but I have to explain. "I was going to cancel, really, but I put it off and she just—"

"I know what *she just.*" Dad sighs and turns the water off. "But what's done is done."

This is one of his mediation-speak lines that doesn't mean much, except that it's time to drop the subject, which he does—when he leaves the room.

"So, what're you girls doing with the rest of your night?" my mom asks. She has her I'm-just-one-of-the-girls tone on. Part of me is relieved because I know my mother well enough to understand she wants things to work out, but the other part of me feels denied somehow. Like instead of me and Alexa against the world, Alexa's slowly being absorbed into my house. "How about a game?" She looks at me and switches gears. "Or maybe we could paint the basement?" It's half suggestion, half question, and I know she means for it to be a nice offering, but it's like wanting a real race car for Christmas and getting a Matchbox.

"Painting the basement isn't the same as painting a canvas," I say. The dishes are soaking in hot soapy water. Twenty-four hours ago, I was telling my family about Alexa. Now she's here and it doesn't feel as different as I thought. Change always seems huge, like your world will morph beyond recognition, the stairs will be where the

138

doors were, the ground lifted to sky level. But it's not like that at all. Instead, there are small shifts—maybe just seats rearranged at the dinner table, glances, and currents of connections.

"We're going out," I say.

"Can I come?" Russ asks. I should have known he would be the first to break. He's a softie, plus Alexa's got the kind of looks that make guys do double takes.

"Sure," Alexa says before I can tell him no. Then I think back to something she said on the phone about how all the guys at her school in Manhattan were pompous, stuck-up jerks. Russ is anything but that. Alexa wouldn't go after him, would she? I shake my head at my paranoia and step in.

"Not tonight, Russ," I say, and note that Alexa seems disappointed. Maybe my paranoia isn't without merit.

My father continues to ignore me and Alexa and our plans, and points toward the ceiling. "The attic. You said you'd get to it tonight, son. You can't put it off much longer. We're running out of space as it is." The attic is an entire floor dedicated to sporting equipment castoffs: cleats, sneakers with the heels worn half down, football helmets that don't fit, baseball pants with permanently spoiled knees, pads, skates, sticks—enough to outfit a village. My dad probably wants to get it organized and donate stuff to the town auction. My mom disappears into the kitchen for a minute.

"You guys could help?" Russ puts on his nice-guy face, his mouth turned up, his eyes like a basset hound.

Alexa looks tempted. "No way," I laugh. "None of that stuff's mine. And you know I'm not exaggerating."

Russ glances at Alexa in a way he hadn't during dinner. There's more intensity in his eyes, and Alexa is kind of reciprocating it. "Thanks for the invite, Alexa." Then he turns to me. "Maybe we'll hang out some other time."

It sounds silly, but I've never really thought much about hanging out with Russ. About being his friend. I've always thought that he's on one side of a line that doesn't really exist, and I'm on the other. Male-female. Brother-sister. Team-alone. Sports-arts. It could be I've been selling us both short. "Maybe," I say to him.

When my mother returns from the kitchen, she hands me a note, and I tug Alexa out the door, leaving the rest of the family behind.

"So," I say when we're outside in the dark. The air is shifting, too, bringing small changes that signal one season giving way to the next. "You ready to go out?" I expect she's going to laugh and say sure, or just hop in the car and fiddle with the radio again.

But instead, she looks up at the house, at the light that's just been switched on in the attic. "I wouldn't have minded helping your brother up there. He's really . . . something."

Suddenly those small changes feel huge. A gust of cool wind marks yet another day lost, and Alexa's comment makes it clear that while we might be linked, we are not necessarily playing on the same team.

TWENTY-ONE

"Jenny's more like a thoughtful chewer—you know, a hangnail puller or something. I'm more of a thorough gnawer myself."

Alexa expounds on our different nervous habits while Tate and I watch her get ready to putt. It's around 9 p.m., so the families with kids who usually crowd Golf on the Green aren't around. There's only the three of us and some scattered couples wandering through the course, putting into windmills and over goldfish ponds, wearing down the already trod-upon fake grass. Earlier we posed for a picture, the three of us dwarfing a tacky papier-mâché gorilla that's seen better days.

Alexa slides her sandaled feet across a bridge that's meant to look like bamboo, her legs long enough to cause momentary envy from me, even though the envy is accompanied by a smattering of self-loathing. I never want to be one of those girls who wishes she were like someone else, or who looks in the mirror with contempt and longing. But when I glance at my pale thighs in the glow from the tiki torches and back at Alexa, it occurs to me that maybe if things were different, like if she lived here for instance, we might not even run in the same crowd. And how weird would that be?

Tate is third to putt. He hangs back and keeps score with a miniature red pencil. "Under par! Nice one, Alexa," he enthuses, jotting down her number of strokes and smiling.

I want so much to take Tate's hand, but I restrain my impulse and shove my hands into my pockets instead, afraid I'll look too cloying or needy. A crinkling sound makes me fidget for the paper in my pocket. It's some money and a note from my mother. *Jenny, Treat everyone to ice cream from us. We love you. Mom. P.S. Be careful!*

She wrote *us* and *we,* but I know my dad had no part in this. She doesn't explain why I should be careful or with whom. Alexa? Or Tate? Or just with my own feelings? I smooth the note out and fold it, then put it back into the darkness of my pocket.

"Earth to Jenny? Tune in, Fitz." Tate twists my nose as if it's a radio dial, which causes me to wince and push his hand away. "Oh, good, you're still with us. It's your turn."

I line my feet up and check out the hole. It's a double one where you have to get the ball in on one level and then again after it sinks through a tunnel and onto a smaller patch of green below. "I'm here," I say. "Just thinking." I take a practice swing. Alexa laughs.

"You're prepping for mini golf?" she asks. She means it as a joke, but it stings a little, especially when Tate cracks up.

"Maybe she's painting in her head?" Tate asks. I despise being spoken about in the third person when I'm right there, but I suck it up, swing, and tap the ball. I will it to be impressive, like in a movie when the girl who isn't athletic suddenly creams everyone else. But the ball moves only a few inches.

"That didn't work," Alexa says with a frown. "You should be allowed a do-over. Don't you think, T?"

My shoulders slump. T? She's got a nickname for him. "I don't need an extra putt. Just go," I mumble.

Alexa steps forward, drops her bright pink ball onto the starting pad, and with hardly a glance, takes her shot. She peers down to see where the ball came out. "Not quite a hole in one, but close. You get that, T? That's two for me."

Tate writes her score down, then takes his turn. We don't seem to be following any kind of order. Maybe this is symbolic. I want him to be affectionate with me. Even though I usually don't like PDA, I could use it now.

"Want to help me line up my shot?" I ask Tate, faux flirting and hoping he'll come up behind me and press against me as he demonstrates the right way to swing.

"You can do it, Fitz," he says, forever encouraging, as he waits for me to take my turn so he can complete the round.

It takes me not three, not six, but ten strokes to get through the fake volcano hole. When I emerge on the other side of it, the prerecorded sounds of lava roaring in the background, Tate and Alexa are in hysterics. Her lithe body is folded over, her hand on his arm to steady herself. My face feels hot with anxiety. First Russ, now Tate?

"Alexa wants ice cream after this. You game?" Tate asks me. He's not fawning over her, but it's so easy to picture him liking Alexa. She is so his type.

I feel sick.

I shrug and commit only to *maybe*. Tate wanders over to the mermaid fountain at the seventeeth hole, takes off his shoes, and puts his bare feet in. Underneath the water his skin appears luminescent and otherworldly. When I watch him chat with Alexa, her theatrics aided by her long limbs and toned figure, I feel that unfastened feeling inside, that Tate will never fully be mine. That there's a part of him I can't ever relate to, the guy in the varsity jacket in the hall-way at school, the MVP hefted onto his teammates' shoulders, the ultracool guy who gets the shiniest girl. The girl who gets a hole in one, like Alexa does on the last hole.

"Where'd you find her?" Tate cracks up while Alexa shows him in slow-motion her perfect swing.

"On the Internet," I say seriously, which makes them both heave with laughter. They laugh so much that I start giggling, too. Then I put my feet in the fountain and Tate puts his foot on mine under the water. It feels cool and soft, as if we're swimming and no one else can see us.

Just as I'm relaxing into his touch—it's the first time we've touched all night—he points to a sign and says, "Hey, Lex! You get a free round. We all do. See?"

Alexa reads the sign, too. "Sign me up! I never say no to free."

I glance at my watch. Another eighteen holes will take a long time, especially with how I'm putting. Alexa eyes me as I hold my putter passively. Tate jumps up on the stone bench and checks out the first hole. "If we go now, we won't have to wait."

Alexa jumps up where Tate is standing, and I watch my own feet, alone now in the little pond. Suddenly, having my skin in the water feels gross. Who knows what kids spit in here or what bacteria lurks underneath? I take my foot out and shake it off.

"You okay, Jenny?" Alexa asks while looking down at me. It's like she and Tate are in the bleachers and I'm on the field with no tricks to show off.

"Yeah, I'm fine," I say. "So, do you guys want to get ice cream? Luscious Licks is open."

Tate nods. "The guys are there, too. We could meet up with them."

Guys is shorthand for the football team, also known as the people who would normally not share a lunch table with me. Granted, more than half the time at school, Faye concocts some interesting and unique sandwich and brings two—one for her, one for me—to the art rooms so I can paint while eating and she can discuss the ingredients. But if I did go to the dreaded cafeteria more often, I sure as hell wouldn't be one of the girls at the player tables (player tables being the sports section of the cavernous lunchroom).

Thinking about the colors of the cafeteria, seeing people's shirts as dots of blue and orange, red and black forms a picture in my mind. I could paint that—a rectangle of the communal tables at schools, how speckled the lunchroom is, how different it is from right now, when I see only two faces in front of me.

"You both look like a painting," I say, trying to be in the moment and not live only in my head. "Maybe I'd use a dark blue background." I look at the sky, taking in the fake glare from the tinted tiki torches. "With a hint of red here and there."

Tate's eyes light up. "Wow, we are witnessing a moment of inspiration!"

"You are not," I say, reaching up to poke him in the stomach. I need that physical contact right now, some proof he's still mine. Or will be.

Alexa smiles. "I'm going to side with Tate on this one, Jenny. That sounded like a great idea for a painting."

I look down at my wet feet. She should be siding with me.

"Maybe you should run with it, you know? Right now, while it's fresh in your mind." Tate is trying to be supportive, but it feels all wrong. He should want me near him.

"Oh yeah? Just where am I going to run with it? In my unventilated closet? No thanks."

"What about Downtown?" Tate asks. He looks at Alexa and explains, "Her studio is over there." He points diagonally from where we are, across the lamplighted street and behind the still-full summer trees to the brick building.

"I don't know," I say. "Sid only lets a couple people paint there after hours."

"That's neither here nor there, Fitz," Tate says playfully as he and Alexa step down from the bench and face me.

Alexa puts her putter across her chest, which just accentuates her assets. "How about this? We escort you to the studios and make sure you can get in and paint the world's best painting ever. Then I drag your boyfriend to go get ice cream with the guys?" She checks out Tate's reaction. "Or we could hang here and putt while you paint."

Alexa's sentences are so problematic I don't know where to begin. How can she use superlatives when referring to my paintings, which not only aren't the "best," but right now aren't even completed? And now Tate has heard that he's my boyfriend—from a third party—when he hasn't even called himself that, at least not to my knowledge. And then there's the underlying problem of my gorgeous new half sister going for ice cream with my could-be-maybe-unclarified-boyfriend while I'm cloistered away in the paint annex. And said ice cream jaunt would be with Tate's crew, who might not know about my presence in his life. It feels weird to think about their seeing Tate with Alexa and not with me. Or worse, the two of them flirting and putting together without me to chaperone.

"There's got to be a way for us to sneak in," Alexa says. She rubs her hands together even though the night is warm. I suddenly flash forward to fall, winter even, and try to imagine where we'll all be when it's cold. Only I can't quite see that far ahead.

"I could scale the wall or something." Tate sounds the most jocklike he ever has with me. Maybe it's Alexa, or maybe it's the thought of performing heroic tasks, but he looks ready to rumble, and not in a way that's appealing. More in the way that reminds me of all the things I am not. Yearbook candids insert themselves into my brain, bringing a vision of Tate lifted shoulder-high, and another of him with his arm around a cheerleader.

"You guys are way too dramatic." I point to the studio building. "Sorry to debunk your breaking and entering fantasy, but it's not locked. Sid Sleethly keeps a brick wedged into the back door so that the special night owls can get in." I think about how Sid gets fifteen percent of the commission for displaying and selling these artists' pieces. I'd give him twenty if I could just have my work on display.

Alexa takes our putters back to the golf shack while Tate pulls me by both hands toward the path that leads across the green to the crosswalk that bridges the road to the studio.

"Come on, Fitz, I know how much you want to get into that art show." Tate smiles at me and I grip his hands tighter.

Alexa catches up with us, sticking close to my side. We look at each other quickly, just enough to lock eyes and smirk. It's impossible to imagine that I didn't know her before, which I guess is that sisterly thing creeping in somewhere.

With each footstep I think about what I'd write on the message board at the donor sibling site: *I met her, and we clicked.* No, that doesn't sound right. How about, *Since you can't guess what meeting your sib is going to be like, you may as well just jump in and find out.* Which I guess is what I've done, only meeting Alexa in person is more fluid than a jump. It's like that weird feeling of being on a diving board, when you're nearly on tiptoe and know you're about to go into the water but haven't yet. When you don't have any clue how it will all work out.

True to my memory, the heavy back door is propped open with an oversized brick.

"I don't know, guys," I say. "What if Sid catches me here and I get yelled at?"

"Are you twelve?" Alexa asks mockingly. Sometimes her comments carry a pinch that continues to sting after the words have faded. She doesn't realize it.

"I just don't want to lose my privileges here." I kick at the ground and bite my lip.

"Most likely, you won't," Tate says. "Right?"

I sigh. If I were alone right now, sneaking in wouldn't feel so weird. I'd just suck it up and say inspiration came to me and voilà, here I am. But with my enablers, I feel like I'm part of a truth or dare game gone awry. Well, not awry quite yet, but on its way.

I take a step toward the door and Tate follows close enough that I can feel his breath on the back of my neck. Part of me wants to turn around and kiss him right in front of Alexa, and I pause, about to do it, but then I stop. Public pawing has ownership attached, and Tate and I don't have the history. I hope we will soon. Plus, a part of me thinks Alexa has the same competitive spirit my parents say I lack. I feel bad even thinking it, but a part of me wonders if she'd try to sway Tate's attention toward her. Still, it's like what Tate said about getting in trouble here: that probably won't happen. But you never know.

Inside, the dank entryway echoes with our footsteps, and I cringe when Alexa sneezes. Then when she looks at me, we get that laughter rising, like in church or in an assembly when you know you can't laugh, and it makes it worse.

"No, wait, shhhh," I say, choking back the laughter.

"I can't." Alexa puts her hand over her mouth, but the

laughter leaks out until we're both clutching each other and shaking. Happy tears form in my eyes, and Alexa finally guffaws so loudly it's not worth hiding anymore. All worries of her competitive streak wash away as she pulls me up the stairs. "If we get busted, just blame it on me, okay?" she says. "I can take the heat."

My heart feels full. I have Tate, whom I've lusted after and pined for for years, trailing behind me, and my sister in front of me. I take his hand and squeeze it, and he squeezes back. But then, right when I'm ensconced in the good feeling of having them both on my side, Alexa stares at Tate, and rather than holding me still, he drops my hand right away.

"You know what it's like?" I say to Alexa when Tate's in the bathroom at the studio and she and I are in the back stairwell, our voices echoing even though we're whispering. I want to convey to her how much I like Tate, just in case she's moving in on him, but I can't.

"What?" She scratches her leg, causing her hair to spill out from its bun. The effect is stunning, and when she stands up, I'm amazed that the first thing I noticed when I saw her in the driveway wasn't how beautiful she is.

"It's like we knew each other before." The metal railing is cold, and I hold it with my right hand while balancing on the balls of my feet on the top step. Alexa leans on the concrete wall and looks at me. In the dim light I think we resemble each other more. In art class this coming year, I know one of the advanced techniques we're learning is how to draw profiles by using an angled mirror. I flash forward to being at school, drawing my face from the side, the class bell ringing in the corridor. Will the profile be mine or look like Alexa's? And who is waiting for me in the hall?

"Oh, I totally know what you mean," Alexa says. Her voice holds excitement in it, the pitch high. "It's like we went to camp together when we were seven. Or you were in my playgroup as a kid. Somewhere we knew each other. And now we meet again."

"A re-meet."

"Re-meet? That's not a word," she says.

"I know, but isn't that what it feels like? Familiar? But not."

Alexa is in the middle of nodding in agreement with me when Tate opens the heavy door and holds it open so I'll go inside. "Your chariot awaits," he says. "If paint supplies can be construed as a vehicle."

I prop the door open with my butt so he can get by. Alexa takes a few steps backward as if she's ready to leave. I wish it didn't feel weird. If Sierra or Sage went out with Tate for ice cream, and they were older, it wouldn't feel bizarre at all. But here, in the half-light of the stairwell, in hushed voices, with me about to go off alone to paint and the two of them about to head out into one of our last summer nights to hang out with friends and drink frothy root beer floats, it does.

"We'll be back in an hour, okay?" Tate says. "I'll show your sister a good time."

"Oh yeah?" I hope I sound breezy and not worried about the potential implications of this. In songs, a good time is always a euphemism for, well, nothing I want to have happen with Tate and Alexa.

"I'll introduce her around." Tate swipes his hand through his hair, a move that always makes me ripple inside.

"If you hurry, you can meet us," Alexa says with gusto. "So get inspired! Think about . . ." She takes the steps two at a time, not bothering to finish her sentence until she and Tate are one flight down. "Think about us!"

TWENTY-TWO

The next two days slide by like trees when you're driving on a highway; sometimes they're a fast blur, and other times, when you're coming to an exit, slow-moving and defined. My dad's been distant with me and Alexa, and my mom's been pecking at us with snacks and chitchat. The twins have become infatuated with Alexa in a way they never have been with me. Her dance ability and paint-free clothing help. Russ keeps up his bravado, but he has been won over by her, too, even lending her his sacred team sweatshirt when she got cold as we strolled around the neighborhood.

I'm still on a high from the artistic charge of completing not one half, but one whole painting the other night. I think about the canvas as I help unload the car. Utopia Lake is crowded today—everyone knows how few mornings and afternoons are left for this kind of outing. Three days until the art show now, two until Sid makes his decisions, and only a handful more before school's in session and I have to face the hallways, with or without Tate.

At the lake, brightly colored coolers flank the picnic tables, wide umbrellas are perched in the sand, and I long for my sketchbook while the rest of the group begins to wade into the water.

"You coming?" Alexa asks. Her yellow bikini is bright as a sunflower against the placid lake. She sheds her shorts right away, ditching hanging out for splashing.

"Maybe in a few . . ." I don't even say *minutes* before she dives underwater and swims with Russ out to one of the rafts. The twins are nearly synchronized in their swimming, and Dad watches them from the shore, his feet in the water.

I sit on a blue-and-white-striped blanket, having organized the food and plates. The chirping crickets hush, and the slight breeze sweeps over my legs until I feel a chill prick the back of my neck. I want to go stand next to my dad, dip my toes in, and slosh around. I want to talk to him about the shades of blue and how I'd paint the water, and ask what he thinks of all this. But I don't. I feel anchored to the blanket.

Hours later I'm half-dazed in the sunshine, while Alexa does backflips across the sand. Sierra and Sage, huddled together under an oversized towel, are captivated by the gymnastics.

"Isn't she awesome?" Sierra asks me, but doesn't expect an answer.

I take a bite of my tuna sandwich and nod, carrying it with me as I wade into the water. Out from shore, my dad swims in circles with my mom, trying to convince me to come in.

"It's warmer than you think!" Dad says, and I wonder if he means the temperature of the lake or his emotional state.

"Come on, honey!" Mom waves, then splashes my dad.

The water laps the sand as I dig my toes in and eat, making me think of blues and greens and other colors that blend but aren't the same. I finish chewing, rinse my hands in the water, and am just about to join my parents when I see Russ at the far end of the beach, talking to someone. My heart slams against my chest when I realize it's Tate—and he's shirtless.

I go back to the picnic blanket and get out the container of cookies and brownies, figuring I'll offer them around. Then Alexa appears, her body glistening with water and her skin tanned. She fluffs her hair back from her face, snags a cookie, and eats it in two bites.

"So good! You never said you could cook!"

"I can't," I admit. "But my friend Faye has great recipes and Mom . . ." But I notice Alexa's not looking at me. Instead, she's focused on Russ and Tate, who are walking this way. Under his arm Russ has an orange Nerf football.

Alexa stands up and waves like a cheerleader. "Chuck it over here!"

Russ and Tate immediately act out a memorized play. Russ throws her the ball, which she catches effortlessly.

"Nice!" Russ yells. "You're a natural!"

Tate concurs, then gives me his trademark grin—his upper lip twists to reveal his bright white teeth. I walk over, and he kisses me—right there on the edge of the lake in front of everyone. Not a major kiss, just a quick one. But still.

"Brownie?" I ask, pointing to the blanket.

"Sure," he says as Russ throws him the ball. "Here, Fitz, go long." He motions for me to run along the sand, which I do, dreading the outcome of this little game.

"Get ready!" Tate yells, pulling his arm back and passing the ball to me.

I stumble on the sand, then quickly recover, and I'm about to actually catch something for the first time. But before I can, Alexa swoops in and nabs the ball, hugging it to her chest. She does it in a smooth and funny way, as if we'd planned it, and we both laugh, as do Russ and Tate. But I wonder if I would have succeeded in catching it if she hadn't intervened.

After a while my parents take the shivering twins back home with Russ so he can continue his attic project. He's been dragging equipment down the stairs at all hours of the day and night, sweat running in rivulets from his hairline. Tate has left with his parents. With everyone else gone, and only the water, cookies, and each other for company, Alexa and I lie down on the blanket.

Facing the sky, we talk and then are quiet, just listening to music from my father's old portable radio, which he generously left behind. She pulls out semi-temporary tattoo paint from her bag. "Want to?"

"Sure," I say. I'm glad we're alone. The whole world seems contained in the square blanket we're sitting on. I draw a small curled motif on her ankle, taking time in my artistry and enjoying it. She does a big smiley face on mine, yellow with a goofy red tongue sticking out of the mouth.

"This is awesome," Alexa says and blows as best she can

on her leg to hasten the drying time. The one I did for her is funky, like one you'd maybe pay for, but the one she did on my ankle looks kind of silly, as if she got bored in the middle and just went for the laughs. I don't say anything, because I don't want to sound critical the way people are of my throwing and catching ability, but I'm a tiny bit disappointed that I'm stuck with this yellow happy face on my leg for the next week. It's just not me.

Alexa admires my handiwork. "You should do one just like this for Tate."

"Really?" I can't imagine why he'd want a twin tattoo to Alexa's, but maybe she's just being funny. I rub at the yellow paint to see if I can wipe it off, but, as the package suggests, it will last awhile.

She shrugs, and one of her tank top straps slips off her shoulder. She has that beach-tousled look, all sun-kissed and glowing. "I didn't mean *just* like it. I meant something just as cool."

I feel better when she says this, but then she adds, "Last night Tate said something about a temporary tattoo he had. A lightning bolt? No, that's not it." She snaps her fingers and nods. "He had a Chinese character that meant 'hard work' or something."

Out on the raft, kids yelp and splash, jumping into the lake while the sun sinks down. My heart sinks, too, with the knowledge that my summery afternoons are dwindling. I can count on two hands the days until that school bell rings. "I read that a lot of the time when people get tattoos of Chinese characters, they actually don't know what they're getting. Some guy thought he had 'man of intellect' inscribed on his arm, and it turned out to be 'oversized brain' or something." I laugh and Alexa smiles, but she stares past me, as if she's remembering something else from last night but not bringing it up. In my head I talk to Faye as if she were here, but she's not—and besides, it's always hard for me to explain my churning feelings.

Later, when we've layered on long sleeves over our suits, we sit on the hood of my car, looking out at the rippling water. I wonder if people who walk past see us as friends or cousins or sisters, but maybe they don't notice us at all.

It doesn't matter, though. We laugh and talk about the things you always think are nothing, but piled up equal a lot. Stories, old crushes, misheard song lyrics, places we want to travel.

"India first, then Australia," Alexa says.

"A tour of great museums," I offer.

The car's hood is still warm from the sun, radiating from underneath as we watch a group of people play volleyball, the white ball still moving in metronomic time. In one of the dry moments when the ball's on the sand, I turn my head to look at Alexa. "Maybe we'd travel together?" I have instant photo-op images of us by European landmarks and at picnics on the beach.

"Yeah. You, me, Tate, and some guy I haven't met yet." Alexa turns her face back to the sky, the sun coating her. "Me, him, the top of the Ferris wheel."

I frown. "Hey, you can't steal my fantasy kiss location." I told her in confidence that I've watched those carnival couples for years and now—finally—I might have the chance to be one at this year's festival. The potential for this has led to some potent daydreams about Tate; the two of us in one of those metal buckets, a rusting fuchsia one or a sparkling blue one that swings back and forth so much it's almost sickening. We wind up at the top of the wheel, looking out at everything and everyone. And then, of course, we share a fantastic kiss that seals our fate as a real campus couple. "Anyway, who would be with you up there?" I cast my hand out to an imaginary Ferris wheel.

"Guess we'll have to see," she says, and licks her lips. My paranoid thoughts about her secretly liking Tate overcome me. "Tate's secret twin brother?"

Her joke hits me flat rather than funny. Why aren't we completely on the same page? She's brought up Tate a lot in the past two days. Apparently, they had a fun time getting ice cream. It was only an hour. An hour and a half at most. Could it have been two? I do some mental math but can't figure it out. Plus, measuring time doesn't always tell you everything you need to know. Tate and I were in school for years, but all it took was one minute of his defending my wet shirt to bolster my crush even more, and his drop-by visit to my house to get us talking. Besides, whatever time they spent together is enough for them to have developed inside jokes and knowing looks and catchphrases like *here comes the dribble* that only reinforce the fact that I missed something.

"I want to go to the studios today. Soon." I tuck my knees to my chest, my feet on the metal bumper. Alexa lies flat, her back on the windshield.

"Tell me about your painting again," she says, and closes her eyes to the sun and spray. No doubt about it—in the

159

movie version of this, she'd be the hot one and I'd be the lesser best friend. I shrug off my negative thoughts and tell her, "It's not bad. Not perfect, but not bad."

"Enough disclaimers. Just describe it."

"Okay. It's bigger than any piece I've done before. And I didn't sketch anything. So there's this technique of wet into wet, where you try to combine things while they're still pliable. Different from letting one layer dry and then adding another. So I used poppy oil to slow the drying time of the paint and the colors—well, you'll see for yourself."

Alexa keeps her eyes closed. "And does this masterpiece have a title?"

"No. I kept trying to think of one, but everything started to sound either lame, like a new lipstick name—*Sunset Surprise*—or else really weird, like *The Science of Being Alone.*"

Alexa turns her face toward me and opens her eyes. The dimming sunlight radiates off her cheeks. "That doesn't sound weird. It sounds good. Did Sid see it?"

"Not yet. At least, he hadn't then. But maybe he has by now." This makes me nervous, and unlike Alexa, who might get bouncy when she's extra worried, I just get worried. Sand sticks to my legs as I hop off the car. "I should go check and see. Will you come to the studios with me?"

I stand up, jingle my keys, look around one last time for anything we might have forgotten near the lake, and wait by the driver's side door, not even thinking for a second that she might want to do something else. But she does.

"I'd rather just hang out at home, if that's okay," she

says, and sits up. When her hair is wet, it looks a shade or two darker, more like mine. Now I think we do look like sisters. The odd thing is, it doesn't make me automatically feel close to her. It makes me want to shoo her away like I do when I find Sierra or Sage in my room without permission.

"Come to the studios." I say it friendly, not whiny.

"Why don't I drive your car, drop you off, and come pick you up in a while. Then we can go do something."

"Like?" Cue visions of sisters in movies—eating cotton candy at some fair, doing a tug-of-war, jogging side by side.

"Like go to Tate's house."

"I think he has practice today." I say it this way to make it sound less defensive, because I *know* he has practice. The red in my cheeks isn't just from the sun.

"Yeah, that's what he said. But someone the other night—who was it? Chris?—said that everyone was going to Tate's house afterward for a party. Or a GT?"

I cough and my expression sours. "Oh, a 'get-together.' " I can't believe I just used air quotes. When did I start doing this? "That's the sports guys' pathetic attempt to keep parents and teachers unapprised of their partying. And they also use this term as a way to exclude people. You know, 'It's only a small GT, not a party or anything. Otherwise, I'd invite you.' " My voice trails off because on one hand, I want to paint and have Alexa there as company, but on the other hand, I want to see exactly what the chemistry is between Tate and Alexa. And because I wouldn't normally be invited to a big GT, let alone a small one.

"Fine. We can go to that later. I just want to make sure I get this done." I demonstrate *this* by swishing my hands around as though each one holds a paintbrush.

We get in the car with Alexa behind the wheel and leave the lake and the last bit of summer behind.

TWENTY-THREE

"You can't go," Dad says with a mouthful of apple. Ever the health nut, he's back from yet another jog in the neighborhood, and the endorphin-filled afterglow he's experiencing doesn't quell his need to control my actions.

"I have to finish the painting if I want a shot at the art show." I rock back and forth on my feet, swaying with impatience. The reality of my time crunch has hit full force today, and I'm a ball of nerves. If I had a team practice, there'd be no question of my attending—Dad would probably even cheer from the bleachers. This gives me an idea, though. Mom had said I never asked anyone to come see my art. Maybe now's the time to do just that.

"Dad? Do you want to drive me to the studios? Then, maybe, uh, you could come up and, um, take a look at my work." I look at the floor. What kind of nervousness is this? It's not like I'm asking him for permission to marry. But then I realize it's the kind of nerves that rear their ugly head when you have a good shot at being turned down. Kind of like last night when the GT at Tate's never materialized and I felt dumb for showing up there with Alexa.

Dad bites the apple again. "Now?" I nod. Dad chews and shakes his head. "Sorry, Jenny."

And right when I'm about to insert a whine–slash–cold shoulder, Dad explains why. "The photographer's due any minute. You need to go change." Dad slips his sneakers off and points to a big cardboard box on the table. "This year we're doing something different." His eyes light up like he's really got a surprise. "How do you feel about purple?"

A few minutes later I'm in my room trying on my standard-issue oversized cotton T-shirt. It's easy to express how I feel about purple. Like crap. Not particularly eloquent, but I'm so annoyed. Every year we do a family portrait. The way some people congregate around the fireplace at the holidays and send cards emblazoned with reindeer and smiling faces, my parents believe in showing our "true colors." This basically means we all wear the same boring shirt, huddle together, and crouch over in our khakis with our thumbs up or some other lame pose while a photographer blinds us with the flash of the camera.

The wall along the staircase is a veritable scrapbook of images—all of us as toddlers in red shirts, then the year when Sierra broke her arm and my parents had the ER docs make the cast match the orange T-shirts, and my personal nonfave, the tie-dye year. For that photo my parents thought it would be funny to have us all make the peace sign.

"Why don't you just say no?" Alexa asks while she watches me groom myself. She wears a bathing suit under a

164

strappy sundress and looks catalog-pretty with her damp hair and summer glow.

"I can't totally opt out of it." The brush sticks in my hair and I pull too hard, wincing as the tangle comes out. I check my watch. "I just have to change, deal with the picture-taking fiasco, and then book to the studios." I look at Alexa's face in the reflection of the mirror. We're standing maybe a foot apart next to one another, and I can see clearly how someone could think we're sisters or cousins, or something. But just as quickly I can see why they'd assume we're not at all related. "I'll be back after I finish, or at least make some progress." I watch her reaction, which is hard to read. "I can pick you up later and we can go to a movie or something."

"So I'm stuck here?" Alexa sighs. It annoys me more than it should. Why should she get to decide exactly how we spend our few days together? It's my car, and I'm the one with a deadline. She can sunbathe here, but if I slack off I'll never get into the show.

"This feels so gross," I say when I pull the purple T-shirt on over my head. "It's a polyester blend and it reeks of sports gear."

Alexa shrugs. "It's not so bad. It reminds me of my field hockey uniform."

My mouth does an involuntary frown. "You play field hockey? In those polyester pleated skirts?" I stick out my tongue so it matches the silly smiley face she painted on my leg. Then I feel bad. "Sorry."

Alexa seems unfazed. "No problem. I get that it's not your thing." She grabs her bag from off the bed, digs out her wallet, and pulls out a picture for me to see. "This was last season. I'm number twelve." In the shot she's midfield, stick down on the still-green grass, her crimson V-neck shirt shining in the autumnal light. Seeing her like that only makes me feel a bigger distance between us. This photo is only a reminder that Alexa is not my twin by any stretch of the imagination, and that this picture would fit better in my family's albums than my recent photos do.

Alexa slicks her hair back into a ponytail and studies me. "Here. Let me do something." She twists the bottom of the T-shirt into a knot that kind of looks like a rose. I look in the mirror. It doesn't morph the outfit into anything glam, but it does make it look less like I shoved my head into a bright iris-colored pillowcase.

"It's an improvement," I say.

Of course, this improvement of sorts is taken as a direct rebellion when we're all assembled in the backyard. The photographer has the lighting board out and the gear all set up, and my father arranges us on the short stone wall in order of height, which puts me in the center, with Russ and my Dad—looking toned and uniform in their purple tops—to my right, and my mom to my left, her shirt tucked neatly into her khaki shorts. Sierra and Sage clearly had access to the shirts a while ago and shrank them so they fit well.

"Undo the knot," my dad says while smiling and looking forward. He glares at Alexa as though he knows she's the one who did it.

"What?" I smile with my top and bottom teeth touching

166

so we can bring this exercise in family fun to a close. *Snap!* Every two seconds the photographer clicks and motions with her hand for us to turn a bit to the side, or else runs over and moves my hand so it's draped across my shoulder or linked through Russ's arm. It's all so artificial.

"Your shirt," Dad says. *Snap!* "It's not right. Everyone else's is tucked in."

"Mine's basically tucked in." I do a quick check of our lineup. "Alexa thought it would look good."

Dad shoots Alexa another mean glare, then leans forward so he can make eye contact with me. "It doesn't."

I sigh and keep smiling. *Snap!* "It's just not that different, Dad." I feel like I have to defend her even though she's been raising my suspicions with her mentions of Tate every two seconds, flicking her wet towel at Russ, and grabbing the twins from their room to dance to a song right when I was about to describe my paintings to them.

"Yeah, Dad, you should be thankful she's wearing it," Sierra says, her smile stretched hammock-wide.

Sage echoes, "And be thankful it's not covered in paint."

"Yet," the twins say in unison.

I glance at Alexa and then back at the twins. That's what I thought I'd have with her—the instinct of fitting together. An innate oneness.

"I think she looks great!" Alexa yells, her hands in megaphone position, from the back door. She stands watching the scene with her arms crossed over her chest. We may not have the oneness down pat, but at least she's in my corner, for now.

"We have a system here," Dad grumbles. The comment

is definitely directed at Alexa. He holds up his hand and signals to the photographer to stop. Then he turns to me and says, "Jenny, just fix your shirt, okay?"

We all know this whole thing isn't about my shirt, but no one says anything else until Russ shoots me a pleading look and whispers, "We're going to be stuck here all day if you keep making an issue of it."

"Russ, I want to get out of here, too. Mom?" I look to her for help.

Mom keeps smiling even though the photographer isn't snapping. "She *is* wearing the shirt, Richard," she says to my dad.

"But not the correct way," he responds.

"I like what Alexa did." My mom touches the shirt-knot. I'm so glad she's on my team for once.

"Well, I like the shirt without it," Dad says without breaking the huddle as he signals to the photographer to start up again.

"Maybe this shirt didn't fit her well." My mom leans on me, which makes me lean on Russ, which causes our whole lineup to bend.

"The shirts are one size fits all." Dad raises his voice for Alexa's benefit. "They don't need any alterations."

Alexa pipes up from the sidelines. "Did you know that 'one size fits all' is untrue? My mom argued that case in a court of law. It's rejectionist. I mean, clearly not everything is going to fit everyone."

Snap! Snap!

"I think we're done here," Dad says, and takes one last look at all of us in our purple shirts—mine just the slightest bit off—and heads to the side of the house to stare for the umpteenth time at his unfinished garden. Then the twins immediately launch into their dance routine, all limbs and flying hair. They call out not to me, but to Alexa.

"Hey, can you show Sage that double-shake thing you did yesterday?" Sierra says. Alexa takes one look at me as if to ask my permission, but she doesn't wait for my response and joins the girls on the lawn.

I head for the driveway, determined to leap into the car and head toward paintville. The purple shirt will be a perfect apron. It will only improve with smears and stains.

"Jenny, hold up a minute," my mom says when my hand is on the sun-heated car door handle.

"Hi, Mom." I open the door to let the bottled-up heat disperse. I know when I get inside, the backs of my thighs will sting on the hot leather. My father always keeps a spare towel in his car for this purpose, but I never remember.

"Dad doesn't mean to drive you crazy." Mom smiles naturally this time. "He's just . . . I think he's a bit out of sorts with your whole . . . thing." She makes a fist and then splays her fingers out like that explains the word *thing*.

"Oh, right, the half *sibling* thing." I overemphasize the sibling part. "Well, I don't know what to say to that. I mean, it's weird enough for me without having to contend with all of you and your reactions." I sigh like I'm being graded on it, regretting the tone of my voice. "Sorry, I don't mean to make it an us-and-them kind of situation."

"I hope you don't see it like that." She pauses. "Then again, sometimes your father and I do put up barriers." She shakes her head but doesn't elaborate. "I know this is tough, Jen. I guess what I'm saying—not that well, of course—is that I understand. Or I'm trying to, anyway." She puts her hands on my shoulders and turns me so I'm facing her. From the backyard I can hear Sierra and Sage laughing with Alexa, the giggles rising into the air like wasps. Mom glances in that direction and then looks at me. "You can't control how people connect."

"Or don't," I add. I hold my breath, picturing the air as a color, all of it housed in my lungs.

Mom nods. "Exactly. You just can't predict it. And maybe Dad likes conformity because it's—"

"Safe?" I suggest, my eyebrows raised. The thought of art is pulling me to the car, to the studios, but hearing Alexa with my family in the yard makes me jealous.

"You're very perceptive." She lets her eyes stay on mine until I look away. "When I decided to have you, I never considered the possibility of your having a sibling out there. Really. It just didn't enter my mind."

"It's a pretty big thing," I say. I mean it in terms of the global reaches of the Donor Sibling Registry, but it comes out as though I mean my life, here, now.

"I'm sure it is. But if you can just try not to force it . . ." She stops herself. "Maybe I should take my own advice." She smiles. "You should go. I know you have work to do."

"I'll be back later to get Alexa."

Mom nods. My father is situated way off near the bags of gravel. He looks over at us and waves. "He's afraid, Jenny."

"Dad? He's, like, impenetrable," I say. I think about him standing in the water at the lake, the blues and greens I never pointed out to him. Then I think about what I would have said about those colors, how they remind me of a river we've been in out in Montana. "Remember Montana? That river?" I recall the scene as clearly as if it's unfolding now. "Dad's the one who stopped me from being carried off in that strong current. When we went fly-fishing? Or, excuse me, when you guys fished and I painted on the riverbank."

My mother wipes her brow where sweat has collected. "He was so worried that you were going to get swept away by the current. And now it's sort of the same feeling. He thinks Alexa's going to try to pull you further away."

"Where? Like to the city?"

Mom's mouth falls into a frown. "Did Alexa already talk to you about it?"

"Talk about what?" I ask, confused.

"She had a chat with us this morning, before you got up." Mom's voice is shaky.

"What about?"

"You should probably talk to Alexa first. Anyway, just know that your father loves you, no matter how it may seem."

I think for a second about my dad grabbing me from the riptide that carried me away from everyone and how he pulled me back. I painted in watercolor then, and gave him a series of rectangular images on thick paper that I never saw again after that trip. That was nearly four months ago.

"We're here for you, Jenny. Maybe we're on the sidelines, but we're here."

I nod, slowly, still thinking about what Alexa might have said to my parents, and take out my keys. Then, when I'm

171

in the car, she knocks on the window. I roll it down part-way. "Yeah?"

Mom puts a palm on the glass. "Go team."

Even though I'm not about to try out for JV anything, nor about to participate in a Fitz-style huddle, even with my purple shirt still knotted at my hip, I feel just a fragment of myself, a puzzle piece, fall into place for the very first time.

TWENTY-FOUR

I read somewhere that twins separated at birth end up giving their dogs the same name, or loving the same music, or painting their bedrooms identical shades of teal. As I drag my paint-laden brush across the canvas, I pause only to wonder if Alexa would choose the same deep shade of blue from the palette or if our semimatching genes have nothing to do with it.

"If you don't overdo it, you just might have something there."

Just as my paint-induced calm is about to emerge, Sid Sleethly's unsettling presence makes my shoulders tighten. He is, after all, the person who could make or break this season's show for me, as well as the spawn of Satan.

"I'm experimenting with wax," I say. "You know, to slow the drying time down." I wish I could retract my words. The guy's a real artist. Of course he knows what wax does to paint.

"Thank you, Jenny Fitzgerald, for that illuminating explanation," he says, and with a sneer he walks away.

I try not to torture myself about the art show. Either I'll get in or I won't, but it's difficult not to try to control it. Or pretend to, as with those irrational games like "If Sid comes back in the next five minutes, then I'll get in," or "If I close my eyes and point to the center of the canvas, then I'll get in, but if I'm too far off, I won't." None of this will solidify anything. And maybe that's what my mother was talking about. There's only so much you can *do*. Some things just happen.

So with that, I keep working on my paintings, moving from one to the next, filling some all the way out to their frame, the colors exploding and leaking off the squares. And in one painting, a small one, I only color the middle, leaving the edges unfinished like a thought.

"That works really well," Jamaica Haas says to me when she glides by with an oversized coffee mug in her hand. "That one." She points to the small canvas.

"Definitely," the man with her says. He's familiar to me, another artist who comes in sometimes and actually sells his pieces. "I'm Vergil Jenkins, by the way. We'll leave you to it."

Vergil Jenkins and Jamaica Haas—two artists who have permanent pieces at the Museum of Modern Art in New York and whose art now sells upward of a college tuition— liked my art. Well, not all of it, just the small one. I study it some more. What made me stop before the edges?

Then it hits me—it's conformity and control. Who says paintings have to go all the way out, that they have to fill their spaces completely? I do another one, this time in yellow that merges into cream. I add twists of brown, curling the paint so it looks leaflike, mottling the canvas, but still I leave a section blank. I think about giving one of them to my dad. I think he'd like it. But then again, I gave him the watercolors from the river that day, and he did nothing with them, so maybe not.

By the time I look up from the three "uncompleted" paintings I've completed, the morning light has shifted to later afternoon. When I see the shadows creeping in the floor-to-ceiling windows, I get a chill. I can flip through the few remaining days of summer like a catalog.

My cell phone ring breaks through my thoughts, and I wipe my hands on a cloth before I reach for it. My purple shirt is not knotted, and the hem hits my thighs, making me look like I'm not wearing any shorts. The purple is no longer pristine. Now it's blotched with paint. But at least it's paint that makes me feel good. Even if the paintings don't make it into the show, I'm happy with them.

Before I check the number on the phone, I think for a moment that maybe my parents are outside and want to come up and see my work—finally. Then I think maybe it's Tate and he's coming up the stairs, and he'll kiss me hello and define what it is we're doing together and what label we'll end summer with. Friends? Boyfriend-girlfriend? Summer fling? Which one?

I flip the phone open and it's not my parents or Tate, but Alexa.

"Hey, are you done yet?"

"I'm just finishing up. They turned out really well. I can't wait to show you. It's like I finally got it, you know?"

"That's awesome!"

I can hear a flurry of noise in the background. "Do you have the TV on?" I ask, picturing her with the twins watching one of their dance show videos.

"No, I'm outside. It's just noisy," she says, and then laughs. "I'll be right there!" she calls to someone on her end.

"Where are you?" I prop the paintings up on the wooden easels in my tiny area of the common room and decide against leaving a note for Sid. He knows they're mine, and a note just seems too pleading, too much like I want to get his reaction (although I do). There's power in letting go, I realize, so I leave my work there, untitled and unsigned, and hope Sid will pick one of them for the show.

Alexa laughs so hard I can't tell what else she's saying. "See you back at the house, okay?" Then she hangs up.

I stare at my baggy T-shirt. Who cares if it's not the most fashionable of fabrics? For once, this shirt has decent associations for me. The day I wore this, I semi–stood up to being different in the face of team Fitz conformity, and most important, today is the day I found my voice, artistically speaking.

I wipe my hands one more time, trying to get the paint off my skin, and then open the back stairwell and go downstairs. I will meet Alexa back at the house, but I deserve a little fun, too, after my hard work. I smile and my heart races when I think about seeing Tate and having him all to myself before heading back home.

The stoplights switch from green to red at the intersection of Lexington Avenue and Rexford Road, better known

176

as the meeting of Lex and Rex. County High is two blocks up on the right, and it blows my mind that we'll all be back there so soon, crammed into the hallways, filtering in the wide front doors with stories of summer that already feel dated.

Driving around town makes me feel like a typical teenager, as if just getting behind the wheel makes me part of a pack. Then again, two of the most common activities of teenage life in this town involve sitting in someone's parked car or sitting at Callahan's. Both of these locations are semi-incidental. We all just need a place to sit and figure out what to do or where to go next.

Faye and I have spent many a night driving from one place to the next, only to avoid Callahan's and go to the Shoreline Diner. Will it be different this year after what's happened with Tate? And what about Alexa? Suddenly it dawns on me that I could visit her in the city, or she could come back. Then I flash to her laugh on the phone earlier and just how chummy she seems with Tate, and I wonder if maybe this visit is our one and only.

The light turns green and I press on the gas, driving through Lex and Rex and up the hill into the more residential area. When I turn onto Tate's street, I'm more than a little surprised to see long rows of cars lining both sides of the road. The gleaming metal bodies of cars with their windows open, the slur of noise in the distance, and the masses making an artful row up to Tate's house clue me in that he's having a party. Maybe this was the GT Alexa mentioned and she had gotten the day wrong.

Now I'm at one of those jock-crowd fetes Faye and I

make fun of. Music filters through speakers Tate or one of his teammates hoisted into the windows. I hear high-pitched laughter coming from a group of girls, the sound of drinks opening, and someone yelling "Bravo!" for a reason I'm not yet aware of.

Never in my imaginings of Alexa, even in my most paranoid state, did I think she'd be calling me on her phone from my boyfriend's house. So when I see her right away, a jolt of panic makes my hands shake uncontrollably. I walk up the steep bluestone path and curve around the side of the house to the large yard in the back. It's so odd to be back here under these circumstances. Tate's house is where we first kissed, and where I first sat down in front of a screen that led me to Alexa, who stands in front of me now.

"Let's go!" Alexa says to me, like it's no big deal she knew about this party and said she'd meet me at home. She gives me the kind of hug that's from the side. It feels like we're about to do a three-legged race and stumble. She's whipped her hair into a messy ponytail that makes her look even prettier than she did today while sunbathing. Alexa is not boring, standard pretty—she's more sleepy and sexy, with cat-lidded eyes and a way of looking at you a little longer than normal, which you'd think would be weird but instead makes you feel special, like you've earned her attentive gaze.

I noticed her looking at Tate this way by the fountain and again at the lake when he did the drop-by at our family picnic. I wonder what kinds of looks I give, even though I know I'll never find out; it's impossible to look at yourself objectively, or maybe to know what effect a certain look has on someone.

"Why didn't you tell me you were here?" I ask.

"Didn't I?" Alexa looks distracted. "That's the reason I called."

"No," I say. "You said to meet you at home. How'd you even get here?"

Alexa shrugs. "Don't make it into a thing, Jenny," she says. "Tate swung by and got me."

I stand there in shock, hating that I can't handle surprises but hating more that these two people I want to trust aren't exactly making me comfortable. "You should've told me."

"Sorry. Don't be mad!" Alexa touches my back gently, as if she really means it, but then just as quickly adds, "Check it out!" Alexa claps her hands. "Slip 'n Slide! How retro cool is that?" The landscaped lawn has a steep incline that lends itself perfectly to the Wham-O Big Splash Slip 'n Slide. Two of them are set up side by side.

"It's pretty standard fare, don't you think?"

"Don't sound so jaded," she says. "In the city no one has yards, right? So hauling butt on a rubber mat outside isn't going to happen." I wonder if she's been here long, what's happened that I've missed. "Speaking of city life," Alexa says, and pulls my arm so we're headed directly for the backyard. "Did your parents talk to you?"

My mind flashes back to the conversation with my mother in the driveway.

"I spoke with them this morning," Alexa says. I glance over her shoulder and see how the cheerleader queens are checking her out. They probably view her as competition. Then I realize I'm wearing my ultradorky purple shirt, which still looks like a lame minidress.

"Do the twisty thing, Alexa."

Alexa understands what I mean right away and starts putting one end into a knot. "So, our chat didn't go over that well."

"Why?" I look down at my shirt, hoping to feel the powerful vibes of finishing my art and the inspiration that came with it, but the studio feels far removed from the suburban wash of tanned girls and guys in end-of-summer party mode. I try to look for Tate without drawing attention to my scanning.

"I guess your parents are not psyched about me."

I look at Alexa, her bottom lip out in a pout. "It's not that they don't like you—"

"It's not like I *have* to be liked or anything," she interrupts, but I can tell from her voice that she isn't telling the truth. Alexa is used to having swarms of kids, adults, even my gawky twin sisters admire her. So it must be really weird for her to come into my family—a family that's kind of connected to hers—and find that my parents (mostly my dad) don't want to accept her. "It's just that they didn't like my idea of you coming to stay with me and my moms in the city for a semester."

"What?" I have to shade my eyes with my hand to see Alexa's face. She's serious. No wonder my dad's even further deranged than before. "You talked with them about something like that without asking me?"

She puts her hand on my shoulder, squeezing firmly. "I'm

only here for a couple more days." She looks over to where Tate is and then back at me. "But wouldn't it be great if we could have an extended visit and you stayed in New York for a few months? The high school art programs are top-notch, too."

When I watch her gaze drifting out to the lawn at Tate, who's surrounded by a group of his friends, I think maybe it's a good thing she's not a permanent fixture in my day-to-day life. But then again, maybe she's right. Maybe an extended visit in New York would be amazing.

If I could just express my doubts to her it would be so much easier, and the weight would be lifted. But I can't; somewhere in my mind, calling attention to an issue only cements the problem's existence. "So, what exactly did you say to my parents?"

Alexa smiles and pulls me toward Tate. "Exactly what I just told you." She blushes. "It was just an impulse. Once I get an idea stuck in my head, I can't let it go."

I yank her arm so she stops moving, and I raise my eyebrows. I wonder what other ideas she has in her head that she can't drop. "But I'm happy where I am."

"Are you really?" she asks as if she already knows the answer.

It's amazing how just a few sentences can cause so much upheaval. No wonder my dad is scared, like my mom said. He probably thinks I'm going to beg and plead to live in the city, just because Alexa wants it to happen. Granted, that would have its pluses: seeing Alexa in her home court, getting to know her better, experiencing a life other than my own. Me in a whole new context. The museums and art opportunities would be incredible. But there would be one big thing missing—Tate.

"You haven't even thought it through," I say firmly.

"It was just a suggestion," she says, her voice edged with cold.

"Well, I can't even contemplate that right now," I say.

Alexa tosses her ponytail and laughs. "Fine. Let's just forget I said anything, have fun, and enjoy the end of summer, okay?"

"I guess." I wish I had Alexa's ability to forget things or jump into things, leaving caution behind.

At the top of the Slip 'n Slide, Tate is damp and shirtless—a combination that makes my normal reaction to him even more intense. He touches my shoulder as a hello and waves ripple in my stomach. Not sick waves, but like parts of me have spilled out and might be on display for everyone to see.

"Hey, Fitz, glad you could maaaaaake it!" Tate's fingers leave my shoulder as one of his teammates pushes him and he slips and slides down the hill and nearly out of sight. His teammates look over, and I think I catch Dan Donovan, Tate's best friend, raise his eyebrows in surprise. But maybe I'm just imagining things. I wish I were wearing anything other than my Fitz family T-shirt, which comes complete with a name and number on the back.

"I'm going next," Alexa says and sheds her shirt, revealing her bikini-clad chest. The act does not go unnoticed by Dan Donovan and Dan's girlfriend, Heather, who rolls her eyes the way all girls do when a pretty stranger inserts herself into the crowd. Alexa leaps onto the slide and goes barreling down, laughing while her ponytail flaps.

"Who's your friend?" Dan asks while sipping a beverage of unknown origin from a tall plastic glass. It's the color blue of the paint I used today. Thinking this brings a small bit of peace to the frenzied scene.

"Yeah, who *is* your friend?" Heather asks, one hand on her hip, the other on Dan territorially.

"She's . . . ," I start. It shouldn't be difficult to iterate, but it is. "She's my sister."

"I thought your sisters were younger," Dan says.

"They are." I sigh and pull at my shirt. The neck is too tight, the fabric lets no air in, and I'm sweating while watching my sister flirt with Tate at the bottom of the slide. They aren't out of view anymore; rather they are walking up the hill together, often leaning in to whisper.

Heather points to Alexa. "So that's another sister? She looks like Russ."

Everyone knows Russ. He's the golden-boy-to-be, I guess, with his charm and athletic grace. "Alexa isn't *his* sister, though."

Heather makes a face as though I'm making this up as I go along. "You're sure you're related to her?" I swear I see her do a double-take of Alexa's features and mine. It's not that I'm unattractive and Alexa's a retouched photo; we're just different. The fullness of this word encompasses the moment.

"I'm sure," I say to Heather and Dan as Alexa and Tate approach. I just don't clarify how. Aside from Alexa, all the girlfriends of the jocks, cheerleaders, and other preppy sportsters are noticeably dry.

"That was splendid," Alexa says. Only someone so shiny-pretty can say *splendid* without sounding like an affected ass. If Faye were here, she'd give me a knowing look.

Tate glances at me, and I can't tell if he's blushing or getting sunburned. What were he and Alexa just talking about? "Yeah, it's great. You should try it, Fitz."

I feel Heather and Dan watch me while Alexa and Tate stand there, waiting for me to make a move. I feel like I'm in the truth-or-dare zone. Where is the quiet Tate, the one with interesting questions and an odd sense of humor? I feel the urge to reach for his hand, but he beats me to it.

"Go for it," Tate says, and pulls me by the hand so I'm right at the top of the slide.

"I'm not in a suit," I say, and tug at my horribly bright T-shirt as proof.

"Who cares?" Alexa says, and pushes my back. Her touch takes away the fact that Tate, in front of all his friends, had reached for my hand. Now it looks like everyone's plotting to get me down the slide and he's just the instigator.

"Hey," one of Tate's teammates says, and points at me. "Is that Fitz's sister?"

This is all it takes for me to perch on the top of the slide, get sprayed by a gaggle of girls who are acting as spraymasters, and ready myself for the long journey down the hill. Tate claps his hands in a show of solidarity. He hasn't made one real nod toward our romance, but I try to tell myself his steady look says it all.

"Here I go!" I say with more dramatic flair than normal. Except, I don't. The water from the hose succeeds only in drenching my ugly shirt and matting my hair. With shorts on I go nowhere, and as soon as my failed Slip 'n Slide action registers with the onlookers, they disperse in search of chips, drinks, and something that actually happens.

"I'll go for you," Alexa says, and hops next to me. In one swift swoop she's gone down the hill, bumping and rolling away from me. Tate stands next to me, his feet near but not touching mine. I wish he'd kiss me, but instead he does an enigmatic tug on my hair and grins.

"I'm glad you're here," he says, and my instant response is a smile that matches his. Tate flips his soaking wet hair back from his face. How is it possible that in private, in the studio, by the dolphin fountain, and in my backyard I've combed my hands through that hair, and now—in plain view of everyone I go to school with, who has seen me pre-braces, with braces, and now without them—I can't even reach for his hand? I'm about to do it, to reach for his hand and not care what the fallout is, when he adds, "And your sister rocks!"

I want to say *half sister*, but I'd sound jealous. Plus, as I stand there wondering about Alexa, wondering what Tate refers to me as in his own mind—friend, girlfriend, Russ's sister—I realize that that the label alone doesn't sum it all up. It's the connection under the title, beneath the summary, that matters.

TWENTY-FIVE

Later that night, when my parents are settled in with the newspaper and Alexa's e-mailing her mothers, the doorbell rings. I'm hardly down the stairs to greet Tate when Alexa shouts from the bedroom, "I'm researching transfer policies!"

The girl has a one-track mind.

Tate is wearing running clothes—shorts that swish when he walks and an old T-shirt that makes me want to grab him and kiss him. "Ready for our run?"

"You bet," I say as I trot over to him in my sneakers. I'm glad I acted on impulse a few hours ago and asked him to show me his jogging route tonight.

Outside, Tate starts off slowly, at a fast walk, but I still have to catch up. "I hope I don't wreck your time or anything."

"You're better than you realize," he says, and pushes my lower back so I'm forced to pick up speed.

"At running?" I ask. But Tate doesn't answer. He just grins and motions for me to follow him. On the moonlight-covered path near the wooded area up the road, Tate's feet start moving too quickly to qualify as fast-walking and I have to work to keep up the pace. My heart fills with excitement. Maybe it's because Tate is leading me into the woods and showing me how to slalom run, bending away from the trees. Or maybe it's just because he's near me.

"I can't believe I'm liking this!" I say, breathing hard.

"Don't act so surprised. You could give a guy a complex."

I laugh and dodge a branch.

"So what was Alexa researching?" he asks.

I jog next to Tate, our legs touching every few strides. "Schools with art programs in the city. She has this crazy idea of my coming to stay with her for a semester so we can get to know each other better."

Tate slows down a little, holding back a thick leafy branch so it doesn't swat me. "You think that's a good idea?"

I shrug. "I don't know. I haven't really thought about it yet."

He stops and stares at me. Then I stop, too, my breath coming out jagged and hard. Running with Tate and the idea of jumping in without a thought makes me brash.

In the dark air I ask, "Would you care if I left?"

"Yes," he says, his eyes flickering on my mouth.

And then I do something else without thinking. I put my arms around him, pull my body against his, and kiss him hard, our breath still uneven from running and even more from this.

"Good," I say. And then I lean in again.

Sticking me with the early-morning shift at Downtown Studios is Sid's way of passively asserting his control. Even though I need to perform maid duty in order to earn the studio time, I don't relish the hours spent with a mop, broom, or any other implement of cleaning torture. With aching legs from last night's adventure with Tate, I mop sludge from the concrete floors. A smile creeps onto my face even as I empty trash bins, walking the bags two at a time down the steps and out into the back lot, where, if I heave hard enough, I can get them into the Dumpster.

Inside Downtown, I sneak a look at my plain-edged paintings and feel a rush. Sid still hasn't made a decision about my paintings and the art show, which I try not to take as a sign of anything other than his laziness and self-centered focus on his own piece of art—a series of murals that take up at least one half of the showroom. I should just walk up to him and ask him once and for all. But since my shift required arriving before sunrise and leaving Alexa asleep in my room, I'm more than ready to depart when I check my watch and see that my shift is over.

I dash out to the car, looking into my oversized canvas bag to search for my keys, when I see familiar blue-and-green sneakers in my line of vision: Russ.

"What're you doing here?" I find the keys and snatch them before they can disappear into the abyss of my bag again.

"Oh, the usual. Jogging. And I hear you're turning into a runner, too."

"Jock rumors travel fast," I say, assuming he somehow saw Tate and me last night. "Want a ride home?" I consider asking Russ to come inside the studios since he's here so I can show him my paintings and give him a brief tour. But

Russ probably has other things he'd rather do with his time, and I don't want him to feel obligated.

"No, you go ahead." Russ swats at a fly near his ear. "I need the workout, and besides, I have to swing by Main Street Hardware, anyway."

"Why? Desperate for a new ladder?" I get in the car and roll down the window. Russ pulls his heel to his butt to stretch his leg muscles.

Russ raises his eyebrows. "No, Dad wants to order a slab of marble for the yard." He looks over his shoulder at the plain red brick of the studio building. "Hey, mind if I check out your stuff in there?"

My body responds to this request faster than my mouth, and my hands pull the key out of the ignition and open the door. My legs are halfway out of the car, my feet on the warming pavement, when I say, "Yeah! I'll show you, but they're on the third floor, which, even though it seems high-up, is actually where they stick the lesser-known artists. Or, in my case, the totally unknown ones."

"You're completely unknown," Russ agrees. "But not forever. You should go home and get some breakfast, hang out with Alexa. I'll go for a quick undercover snoop and report back."

It's clear Russ wants to take his inaugural tour alone, and I don't think about asking why until I'm almost home.

The first shocker is that no one is in the front yard when I pull into the driveway. As the countdown to fall has begun,

I figure everyone will be basking in the sun on the few sunny days we have left. But the driveway is vacant.

The next shocker is bigger. When I walk toward the side door, the backyard is filled with laughter: Alexa's and my dad's. As I approach the stone wall that separates the patio from the grass, I can't help but notice Dad's to-be-completed area is cleared out.

With my bag slung over my left shoulder, I move my sunglasses up onto the top of my head to make sure I'm not missing something. Sure enough, not only are the gravel bags gone, but the dumping ground of raw materials is, too. Where just yesterday there was a heap of mulch and upturned flowerpots, now there are planted shrubs.

"Hey!" Alexa is dirt-covered and smiling. She is sitting in a ring of pansies near a tangle of sweet pea blossoms and waving me over.

"Check it out!" Dad gestures with his chin to the stone bench near the edge of this transformed area. I plop down onto the bench, soaking up the cool from the cement and taking in the transformation. I wonder if Russ wanted me to come home now so I could see this. Maybe he knew I'd be bothered, or that at the very least I'd want to know what was going on when I wasn't looking.

"What do you think?" Dad asks, wiping his dirty hands on his pants. He stands up on the patio and hands a bottle of water to Alexa, who swigs from it right away.

Alexa answers before I can. "It's different, isn't it? A huge improvement."

Dad comes over and pours his water onto the pansies. "Alexa suggested a slab of marble for over there." Dad

190

points to a rectangle of uncovered earth, its soil dark against the colorful array of blooms.

"Alexa did?" I say with a chill. How could she suggest this when I left her sleeping upstairs?

"Over breakfast while you were at the studio, she mentioned that she was the head of a city gardening group."

"Yeah, I know," I say. I'm jealous enough of their home improvement scene together that I semispit the words out. "She arranged for all these stores to donate goods, and these kids to volunteer to transform this tire factory space into a usable garden."

"You never told us that," Dad says.

"I didn't?" Maybe I thought I did. Maybe I just assumed those details wouldn't matter to him. Guess I was wrong.

"Anyway, impressive stuff. She sort of inspired us to tackle this thing once and for all." Dad shakes some loose dirt off a shrub and looks at me.

I'm about to nod and smile and reiterate how nice it looks, when I realize this won't help the situation. "You could've waited for me to get back," I say. "I would have helped."

Dad studies my face. "Really?" And then, as if he's doubting my sincerity, he adds, "It was sudden. That's sometimes how these things go."

I want so much to say I feel like I missed out, but it'll sound stupid. I've had the chance to do this garden project all summer, and I've mustered precisely zero interest. It's only now when I'm cut out of the activity, that I realize I want to do it. I stand up and follow the path of bluestones until I'm at the kitchen door. Instead of saying anything, I kick at one of the stones and don't fix it. "It looks great,

Dad," I say, and go inside, leaving him to admire the work, and letting that one imperfect stone stay on its side.

"By the way," he says, "the photographer needs to reshoot this year's family portrait. The lighting was all wrong."

I wince. Dad will be furious if I tell him that I've already ruined the purple shirt. It's covered with paint now. But I nod and decide to put off telling him this. "Um, okay. Just tell me when."

Once I slide the glass door open and step into the dark cool of the kitchen, it dawns on me that maybe it's not that I didn't participate in the beautification of our backyard that really bugs me—maybe it's because Alexa did. I grab a snack and flip though the mail. One letter, overnighted, is for me—a packet of information from some school in New York about the transfer process. The language is complicated, and I read it as Alexa goes by me, up to my room.

A few minutes later I enter my bedroom waving the letter like a flag. "It's too much," I say tersely, the express packet heavy in my hand.

Alexa's on her cell phone, her hands still grubby, and covers the receiver. "Oh, it came? Good. I just wanted you to know about your options. And that's all they are: *options,* right?"

I leave the room again to check on the view of the yard from one of the upstairs windows. It looks nice, truth be told. But I still feel left out. This feeling is exacerbated when I pad quietly down the carpeted hallway and push my now closed bedroom door open with my bare foot and find Alexa still on the phone. I stand there for a minute while she's saying, "She won't know. It's a good cover. Yeah, me too."

The words themselves are cause enough to trigger alarm. Combine them with Alexa's hushed tone and the way she's twirling her hair in her fingers while she talks, and she might as well be standing under a sign that reads I'M DOING SOMETHING SHADY.

But I don't register all this until she sees me and flips her phone closed without so much as a *see ya.*

"Hey!" She's forcing a smile.

"Hey." I slump my bag onto my desk. It's been less fun sharing a room than I thought. Sierra and Sage never complain about cohabiting, but the fun of splitting my space is wearing thin. Alexa's clothes are strewn over most of the floor; her books, pens, multiple swimsuits, and lists are enough to take over the bulk of the square footage. If my closet weren't so fumy and filled with paints, I'd have slept in there.

"That was my mom," Alexa says, still holding her phone so tightly her knuckles are white. "I called her to say hi."

I'm about to shrug off the weird tone when I notice Alexa is biting her top lip, chewing it pensively. Then I panic. When I put my lower teeth on my upper lip like that, it's because I'm distorting the truth or hiding something. Not that I do it often, but it's usually an inadvertent action that indicates I'm covering up, like when Russ first asked me about Alexa, or a couple times this summer when Sid's asked if I triple-swabbed the floors. Or when I didn't tell

Tate how I felt about him and our maybe-future in the gravel stacks, which have now been transformed into a garden. "Really? Your moms? How is she—or they?"

Alexa notices me looking at all her stuff, but doesn't collect the articles of clothing on the floor. "They're good." She looks at me and scratches her nose. "They're really on board with the Jenny Fitzgerald Study Abroad in NYC plan." She raises her eyebrows in the hope I'll be excited, too.

I sigh and twist a piece of my hair.

"What?" Alexa asks, and waits for a response.

"Nothing."

"Okay, well, I hope you'll think about it seriously. A semester in New York would give you so many opportunities. Museums, galleries, and me!" She smiles. "I'm going to shower. Then we can make a plan for the day." She gives me an overdone grin that reminds me of the temporary tattoo on my ankle. When she grabs a towel and heads to the bathroom, I look at the yellow circle on my ankle and wish again that it would leave. Or maybe this is just my way of saying I'm ready for Alexa's departure, too. Not today, but after the carnival and the art show, I think it'll be time.

As I stare at the mess of my room, an idea pops into my head: why not jump in again? If I'm suspicious about her phone call, why not check? I grab Alexa's phone and open it, fully expecting to find her home number on there. I go to the last number dialed; it's not a long-distance area code. It's local. And not just any local number, but one I recognize: Tate's.

TWENTY-SIX

Alexa emerges from the shower twenty minutes later looking clean and rejuvenated while I am silently fuming. My
rationale is this: if she'd come right out with the fact
that she was talking with Tate, maybe I wouldn't feel so
betrayed. But the intimate tone and her secrecy only prove
that she's got something to hide. Her lip-biting was a
true sign.

"So, what are we up to today?" Alexa slides a comb
through her hair, pushing all of it forward onto her face,
and then in one big motion flicks her mane back. She claims
this makes her hair appear fuller. I can't attest to this, but I
can say it does spray water on me.

I wipe my face with my palm and busy myself, hiding my
hurt and anger in menial tasks: straightening books on my
desk, fixing the blinds Alexa left crooked this morning, and
attempting to gather her stray clothing into a heap near her
Aerobed.

While she considers various outfits, Alexa takes in my
tidying. "Are you hinting that I'm a slob?" Her laughter

doesn't lighten my mood; rather, it digs at me. How can she find all this funny? This whole situation is out of hand.

I shrug and keep cleaning, crouching by the built-in bookshelf near my window so I can neaten it up. The thought of textbooks making their way to these shelves in under a week makes my chest hurt, and the thought of walking the same hallways I did last year makes me feel like I'm caught in a loop of life—one season into the next without stopping. I will go back to the same school with the same people and the same ugly maroon chairs that have held countless County behinds over the years—only this time, I'll be different. Suddenly I knock a pile of books off the shelf on purpose, only Alexa thinks it's an accident.

Alexa crouches next to me. *"Wuthering Heights."* She points to the book's spine. "Good book."

"Really?" I'm unable to keep my voice steady. It rises as though I'm about to cry or scream—who knows which one. The whole time I talk I'm really thinking about her, and feeling betrayed, and my tone shows it. "I thought it was overrated. You read all this stuff about how great love is, but does it have to be so tortured? So tragic? In the end I just didn't care that much about Catherine and Heathcliff. The best part of the novel was the description of the landscape." I look away from Alexa and try to control my voice. "The countryside was a whole other character."

This is true. I wasn't caught up in the typical love and longing of that novel, but I read and reread the passages about the moors, the dank grassy hills, and the dark forests. Maybe the images made me think of painting, the textures and richness. Inside, my chest is tight. If Faye were anywhere reachable, I would leave my room to call her or e-mail her. I'd send brain waves if I thought they'd reach her—anything so I could unload my worries and get some perspective.

"Yeah, I could see that," Alexa says, pulling me back to the moment. She waits for me to comment further, but I'm all out of literary discourse. "I'm confused," she says with a strange expression on her face. "Is something wrong?"

I've seen Sage and Sierra go at each other, but despite our bickering or the way Russ and I poke at each other sometimes, I've never really had a heated discussion with my siblings. Or maybe *discussion* is too mild a word for what is about to happen. I knock the stack of books over again that Alexa straightened. "What's wrong is that I can't trust you."

"What?" She looks shocked.

"You know perfectly well what I mean." I start to yell. "You and Tate playing putt-putt and you pushing me to go paint so you could go off with him. Do you know how humiliating it was to show up at his house and find you there? You said you told me, but you didn't. You hid it from me." I grip my hips with both hands and press my feet into the floor as though I need an anchor.

"You're way off the mark, Jenny. I would never . . ." She falters. "I just wanted you to do something." I want to defend myself, but Alexa goes on. "Sure, you tell me about art history and you let me *see* your life, but you don't explain what's really *inside*. Are you so afraid of the fallout that you can't even risk saying anything? You never say what you're really thinking. Until now."

"You want me to talk? Fine. I'll talk. Maybe you're onto something. In fact, I know you are. Yes, I get worried about what will happen if I say what I really feel. If I tell my dad that I'm hurt he did the gardening project with you instead of me, I'd feel dumb. We're different, you and me. You act before you've even thought of the consequences. Did you for one second think that maybe it would be nice if you'd let me work on the garden with my dad—that the *three* of us could have fixed it?"

Alexa looks like she's been slapped. She opens her mouth to say something, but doesn't.

"No, you didn't. Just like you didn't think about stepping over my catch at the beach. Or butting in so I can't possibly be close with Sierra and Sage. And you just insert yourself with Tate and with Russ and with the school stuff." My voice is definitely getting louder.

"I thought you wanted to transfer!" Alexa says sharply.

"No. *You* want me to. It's just another one of your impulses." I take a shaky breath and sit down on my bed while Alexa still stands there in front of me, arms at her sides like a soldier ready for action.

She makes her mouth small and her voice contained, quiet. "Just tell me, right now, exactly why you're so pissed at me."

Outside the window the sunlight flickers, casting shadows on my walls. "When I first found out about you, I was so relieved. Like, here's my chance to have what Sage and Sierra have."

"But we're not twins," she says as if this explains it all.

"Can I finish?" I feel my heart speeding up and twisting.

There's so much doubt in me now—with Alexa, with Tate, with my family, with the art show—but I press forward and test myself to see if I can say what I mean without backing out. "So we're not the same. But that's what I wanted. Or what I thought I wanted. I see my sisters and their amazing way of overlapping—how they flow into one another. And I wanted that. So I'm not mad at you. I'm let down by my own imagination."

My voice trails off, and I study the mist of dust that's illuminated by the streams of sunlight. Then I think about taking all the blame myself, and that doesn't feel right. "But that's not the only thing. It just feels like you need to prove how amazing you are, how much better you could be at being me than I am." Letting the words out of my mouth feels like pulling away at a part of myself. I realize that's exactly what I've been feeling.

Alexa looks at the floor and rests her palms on her knees and doesn't say anything for a minute. "I can see why you'd think that."

I expected her to freak out and yell at me, but she's calm. "Really?"

Alexa nods and looks up at me, then looks down again. "I do that sometimes. I don't know why. I just—" She coughs and brings her knees to her chest. "I'm totally driven and controlling and demanding, and maybe I'm like that here, but even worse."

"But why?" My voice is pleading, and I pick at the paint on my shorts to distract from the intensity.

"Because you have this incredible life here." Alexa sweeps her arm around as if she's describing game show prizes. "Cool sisters who look up to you." I shoot her a look of disbelief. "They do. You just don't know it because you don't talk to them and they're intimidated."

"By me?"

"Um, they're twelve and you're this sensitive brooding artist in the closet. Yeah, they're intimidated by you. And Russ, he's adorable, first of all."

My pulse pounds with this comment because it reminds me of Alexa and her nonboundaries—she can steal Tate, but she can't start in on my brother, too. The tension is so thick I can't breathe.

"He wants to hang with you and you always bag out on him. 'No, you can't come with us. No, I'm not up for volleyball.' " Alexa imitates me with such accuracy I'm embarrassed and angry at the same time.

"I hate volleyball. Ever seen someone who hates bees try to swat them away? That's me with the ball."

"But who the hell cares? You think that's what Russ is asking? He's asking to do something with you, and since you don't hand out a brush and palette, he's offering the bat and ball or whatever."

I hadn't considered this before, and the last thing I want to do is think she's sucked up all this in a week with me, but maybe she has.

Alexa turns away from me and starts folding her clothing briskly into neat stacks worthy of a boutique. "You talk about colors and what they mean and how you use them to convey what you feel in your paintings. But why is saying the words that you need to say to people such a bad thing?

How do you expect to have people know what you want unless you *tell* them?"

Her tensely spoken words rain on me, chilling me to the bone and leaving me angry and upset. "I need some air," I say. She's on one side of the room and I'm on the other. I wait for her to grab me as I walk out of the room, but she just lets me go.

Outside, I sit on the stone bench, hating the way Alexa's pansies have encroached on the rest of the lawn. It's as though even her plants want to take over. I've just always thought that if people really know you, then you don't need to explain what you're thinking and how you're feeling. Inside, I feel that ripping sensation, the hurt that happens when I'm honest with myself. The thing is, after I let the reality seep in, relief follows. I know I've been hard on Alexa—too hard, and I need to say so.

I always think I know how people are feeling, or more what they're thinking, but I don't. I don't really know what Russ feels or what Tate thinks or if Sierra and Sage would talk to me on the way home from camp or if my parents want to have more to do with my art—because I don't ask. I offer little tidbits; the watercolor river series I painted in Montana and gave to my dad was a test, like if he loved me, then he'd love my paintings. But I never saw those river paintings again. And I figure if the twins wanted to talk to me, they would. And if Russ felt like hanging out, he'd clue in that maybe backyard sports isn't going to do it for me.

When you realize you've been wrong, that you've been missing out on parts of your life, the wind leaves your body at an immeasurable rate. You can't get back the unspoken conversations, the afternoons spent thinking instead of explaining yourself, the night of being left out while the rest of your tribe is somewhere else. Suddenly I see my life unfolding fast, like I have the chance to be proactive. Rather than feel crushed by everything I haven't done, I think about what I could do. Not that I'm going to rush out and yell my feelings from the top of the studio, but I could stop building the wall around myself—maybe loosen the mortar that's been drying.

I retrace the steps to my room and know that now's the time for an apology. A real one. Alexa is right where I left her, folding her clothes in a way that shows me she's trying to busy and distract herself. I don't think she expected this bump in the road, either. I clear my throat louder than necessary, and she shifts her gaze to me. I sit on the edge of the bed and take a deep breath. "I'm . . ." I pause and search for the right words. "I'm kind of—"

She stops folding and cuts me off. "Look, it wasn't going to be perfect, right? How could it be?"

I nod and think back to the moment I found her. "I kept checking the message board to see if they'd have the answer to everything." I'm building to an apology, but she won't let me get there.

"I know, I did the same thing."

We stare at each other and I'm aware of Alexa's whole being. We share a biological father, but our daily lives are separate. I want to know what she thinks about me, and

I'm about to do my usual nonasking when I press myself to reach out to the edges of the canvas in our relationship. "Will we always know each other?"

"I want to," Alexa says softly. Her cell phone's ring breaks the hush of the moment. We both look at the phone as it vibrates on my desk. "I should get that, it could be Mom."

"I thought you just spoke with her." My voice turns steely as I recall each word she uttered to Tate. All the revelations I experienced outside are being evacuated from my mind.

Alexa remains calm, but bites her top lip. "Well, sometimes she likes to call back. We miss each other."

"Okay, that's enough," I bark, and stand up, leaving the bed's warmth and any fuzzy feelings I had behind. She's lying right to my face, and I can't let it slide, no matter how much I want to. "Just tell me the truth, Alexa."

"What?"

"I see how you look at Tate, and I heard you on the phone with him, okay? I looked at your phone while you were in the shower and saw his number."

Alexa is staring at me in stunned silence, and the fact that she doesn't come out and admit it is making me even more furious. That she had the gall to lecture me on how I should interact with my family when she can't even be honest with me makes me queasy. My skin feels like it's on fire, so when I continue talking, it sounds as if I'm about to go on a rampage. "It's so pathetic that you have to come here and invade my life and try to win."

Alexa narrows her eyes at me, through being nice and

calm. The phone stops ringing, and when it does, she launches into defensive mode. "Well, I think it's rather pathetic of you to spy on me and invade my *privacy*. Are you that insecure that you'd assume Tate would drop you for me?"

I exhale hard, as if Alexa has socked me in the stomach. Once I regain my composure, I make sure my words hit even harder. "Are you that insecure that you need to steal my family and boyfriend in order to feel important?"

Alexa squares off against me. "Nothing happened with Tate," she says firmly. "And I wasn't trying to steal anything from you."

"Whatever. I saw you flirt with him, and now you're having secret phone calls." I want to drop my anchor in the small epiphany I had minutes earlier, but I'm too angry to hoist it overboard.

Alexa's hands shake. She tries to quell the movement, but I can see the fluttering. "You're totally paranoid. What're you going to say next, Jenny? That I made you go paint that night just so I could get some time alone with him?"

For once, someone has read my mind exactly. I had hoped that someone would be Alexa, but I never dreamed it would have happened like this. "Did you?"

Alexa rolls her eyes and runs her hands through her hair. "All I wanted to do was get to know you through him. Haven't you ever wanted that? To slip into someone else's world and see what it's like?"

The question doesn't even register. I just want her to stay away from Tate, and me, at least for a while. "Stop making excuses. It's pretty clear what you wanted to do."

Alexa knocks over her pile of clothes with a clenched

fist. "I don't like Tate! What do I have to say to get that through to you?"

Her proclamation leaves me absolutely cold. In my head the only thing I can think of is that Shakespeare line, "The lady doth protest too much." "Right now there's nothing you can say."

As I walk out of the room, I notice that tears are streaming down Alexa's face, but it's not until I wander into the bathroom and catch a glimpse of myself in the mirror that I realize tears are streaming down my own.

TWENTY-SEVEN

"Hey," Russ grunts at me in the hallway once I leave the upstairs bathroom. My eyes are still a little red and puffy from crying. I hope he doesn't notice. "Hold this." He has a long, wide piece of wood balanced on the banister, so his mind is completely preoccupied.

"A little light lifting?" I ask as I take one end and he takes the other. My hands aren't even remotely steady, thanks to the fight with Alexa and the worry of not knowing what'll happen with her, my paintings in the art show, and Tate. Why does Faye have to be unreachable at a time like this?

"Try not to drop it, Jen." His forehead is sweat-wet and his face is flushed. "And don't forget to bend your knees."

"Let me guess; this is left over from the brilliant new garden." My heavy sarcasm bothers me, so I try my new technique of saying what I feel. "I'm glad you suggested that I come back and see it."

Russ looks at me across the long plank of wood. "Yeah, I figured you'd want to know. Kind of weird, right? Not like you were so fired up about doing it, but still." He read-justs his grip. "Now, angle it up and back."

Right then I am filled with love for him because he un-derstands. "God, this is incredibly heavy."

"One more heave," Russ says. "By the way, I tried to check out your paintings, but some English dude kicked me out."

"What? Oh, that was probably Sid Sleethly. He's a pompous ass on the outside, and seriously mean on the in-side." I make an evil face. "Thanks for trying to see them. It means a lot, Russ. Really."

"No problem." Russ suddenly lets his end go, and the plank bangs down onto the carpet. His face turns red. "Okay, you can put it down."

But I hold on, hoping he'll let me help him with his proj-ect. "Oh, I'm fine. This thing isn't even heavy." Then, in case he doesn't get what I'm implying, I ask, "Do you want any help up there in the attic?"

Russ pulls hard on my end and lays the wood down flat on the floor. He seems testy all of a sudden, and I haven't the slightest idea why. "I appreciate the offer, but I've got it under control."

I look at his face, seeing a constellation of freckles on his nose. "Hey, I have that same thing." I touch his face, and he flinches, but then touches mine.

"I never noticed before," Russ says.

We stand there for one more second, looking at one an-other and our similar marks, and I see us on canvas—dis-tant at first, and then pulled together, slowly, attached like the stars are, hinged by unseen lines. "You sure I can't bring this to the attic for you?" I raise my eyebrows and try to forget that behind my bedroom door Alexa could be talking to Tate, although that's not humanly possible.

"No, that's okay," Russ says, the stressed-out tone returning to his voice. "I'm sure you and Alexa have other things to do."

"Right," I mumble as I watch Russ carry the plank of wood up to the attic easily without me.

On the patio, Sage and Sierra have two large pieces of cardboard between them and a tray of watercolors. From inside, I can tell they're arguing. Sierra's brow is furrowed, and Sage's mouth is twisted so small it looks like a prune as she tugs on Sierra's paintbrush. I'm about to keep within my boundaries and leave them to their own devices. But then I think about how things went with Russ in the hallway. I asked to get involved in this one small part of his life, and he said no—I felt bad, but not as bad as I thought I might. In fact, it was kind of liberating to just put myself out there and see what would happen instead of assuming things. I may as well try my luck with the twins.

I slide the door open and hear my sisters whining.

"You can't do it that way."

"Shut up! Just give me the brush. It was my idea."

"What's up, guys?" I feel like a teacher interrupting an unsupervised study hall. The twins, surprised by my appearance, scramble to reassemble their work space.

"Oh, hi, Jenny." Sierra lets go of the brush and Sage reels backward. "We're just—"

"Making a sign," Sage says, her voice a little too forceful.

"For what?" The watercolors they're using are drugstore ones. They'll never show up dark enough to be readable.

They exchange a glance and Sierra stutters, "Um, uh . . ."

"For the dance show," Sage says, and looks down.

"Wouldn't the camp handle that?" I ask, and then feel as though they'll take any further questioning as criticism.

"Right, sure," Sierra says. "These are just . . . extra. You don't have to bother with it."

Something feels funny about the twins and the way they're hedging their words. Usually they jump right in and hit me over the head with their projects, but I try to give them the benefit of the doubt. Plus, maybe Alexa was being perceptive when she said the twins are intimidated by me. "Do you want any help?" I ask.

Sierra stands up right away. "No. No. NO."

This second rejection stings much more than I'd like it to. But I know I need to continue to put myself out there to get a response, and not be put off by one *no*—or three. "Okay, maybe some other time, then."

Sage stands up next to Sierra. I can tell that they're taller now than they were at the beginning of the summer, because the shorts they have on were longer on them in June. Sierra's bangs have grown out, and I notice Sage has kept her hair shorter. They don't look as identical. Or maybe that's just my view right now.

"Yeah, some other time," Sierra says, smiling.

The yard seems different to me, too, like the way colors sometimes seem one shade before you paint with them, but change entirely once they dry on the canvas. It's about per-spective, I guess. In the upstairs window I see Alexa's face, her palm pressed to the glass, watching all of us. Although I'm still reeling about her and Tate, I remind myself that our conversation helped me see things about my life a bit more clearly. I look away and back at the twins. "You guys seem different to me. Before, you were so . . ."

"Matching?" Sage finishes off my sentence. I wish I had a video camera to record the moment for posterity. Who knows if it will happen again? "Yeah, it's weird how we just changed, huh?"

"Not really. Change happens when you least expect it."

Sierra takes a tentative step toward me and I think we're about to have a made-for-TV miniseries moment, all huggy with stringed instruments playing in the background. Instead, Sierra points to my shirt. "Nice, by the way."

I look down and see a stripe of bright red from the paint-ing I started last week but never finished. When I think about the ragged-edged ones, the paintings I feel are worthy of being viewed, I see the red stripe as a reminder of what came before, all that unknowing, that fear of what might be or might not be. Red like Tate's lips, a kiss that may or may not happen. "It's called poppy."

"Please don't *ever* borrow my shirts," Sage says. Her laugh is familiar, throaty, and makes me smile.

"You're so shallow." I shake my head.

"And you're so messy," she says.

Then I go for broke. I open my tiny little microcosm of my world up to them. "Listen, if you guys want, feel free to use some of my oil paints. Not the new ones, but any of the tubes in the shoebox." I see the generous comment affect them physically. Sage's eyes grow wide and Sierra's shoulders rise up. "They'll work better than the cheapo drugstore paints."

"Thanks, Niffer!" Sage says excitedly.

My heart almost floats away when she says that. Before she could say Jen, she used to call me Niffer, back when I was the one she looked up to and being a twin hadn't completely dominated.

I feel so much better. Not perfect, but better, like everything that isn't irrevocably broken has the potential to be more than what it is. I can only hope that Alexa and I will be able to pick up the pieces and find out what we are now and what we can be in the future.

But before that can happen, there's something I've got to do first: ask Sid Sleethly a question or two.

As I'm on my way to Downtown Studios, my message alert goes off on my phone. I call in to voice mail, wondering why my phone didn't ring, but then realizing it probably did while I was outside with Sierra and Sage. I listen to a message from Tate. He tells me he's finally done with mandatory team organization, that he walked by the carnival area and it looks great, and that he's psyched to see me soon.

I call him back and ask him to meet me at Downtown—if Sid tells me he didn't pick any of my pieces for the show, it will be good to have someone there to soften the blow. He agrees, and this makes me perk up. Maybe Alexa is right.

Maybe I'm just insecure when it comes to him. I know now that I have to ask him what's going on with us if I'm ever going to feel on sturdy ground.

Tate is in front of the studios when I pull up. I park and walk briskly toward him, desperate to talk with him about us.

"Hi, Jen," he says, his voice sounding detached and weird.

I wait for him to kiss me hello, but he doesn't. All my resolve quickly vanishes—I'm too worried that he's thinking about Alexa. We wind up inside the front door, standing awkwardly together, watching Sid ranting and raving while stomping around.

"It will never be finished at this rate!" he yells, and points to various assistants, all clad head to toe in black. "The printing is behind, the whole left wall needs to be staged, and . . ."

"Excuse me," I say meekly, making Sid aware of my presence. If I wait until things settle down to talk with him, I know I'll lose my nerve.

Sid ignores me and barks more orders.

"Is everything okay?" Tate whispers in my ear.

I'm about to reply when Tate's phone rings. He checks the number, silences the phone, and puts it back in his pocket. I just shake him off and focus on getting Sid's attention. "Sid, I was wondering if I could talk with you about my paintings."

Sid's voice booms out to me. "Can't you see that I'm insanely busy? Of course not. If you don't have artistic vision, why would you have common sense?"

I open my mouth to confront Sid, and Tate's phone rings

again. This time he takes the call, furtively talking into his phone from the corner of the room while I deal with Sid.

"I just wanted to know if you decided to put any of my work in the show. A simple yes or no answer will do. And then I'll be on my way."

"Well, it's hard to decide something like that when you didn't submit anything." He sighs heavily and snaps at another assistant while I absorb what he's just said.

"But I did. I submitted a few pieces, actually. I left them out for you. They were the ones with unfinished edges." My voice is high and squeaky from nerves.

"I don't know what you're talking about. Now, please, go off and make out with your boy toy so I can work," he snaps.

Panic surges through my body. I start up the stairs to the floor where I usually paint, and leave Tate behind as he talks on the phone. On the wooden easels where I last left them, there are dry-mounted posters announcing various "real" artists for the show. And in the little room where I usually paint, there are only stacks of shrink-wrapped, sealed postcards—artists have them printed with a key work of art on the front and their galley representation on the back. I don't see my three paintings with the unfinished edges anywhere. Now true fear rises in me.

I run back down to where Sid is slicing open cardboard boxes with an X-Acto knife. "Excuse me?"

"What now?" he asks.

"I think someone lost my paintings," I warble. I'm about to cry, and the last thing I need is for Sid to see me break down. "I can't find them anywhere."

Sid listens patiently while I stutter along, and then says slowly, "I don't have time for this."

This instantly angers me. How could he be so heartless? I'm about to unleash mayhem on Sid, but I'm cut off by my own cell phone. Sid glares at me again. Just then I realize Tate has left the building. Sid points to the ringing phone as if it were vermin and then to the door.

I dash outside, squinting in the sudden brightness. "Hello?"

"Hey!" my long-lost friend Faye says. "I won a bake-off challenge and the prize was phone privileges!"

"Thank God you called."

Then I explain it all to her from the beginning.

TWENTY-EIGHT

Talking with Faye for about fifteen minutes has given me temporary relief. All these worries about my missing art-work, my pseudo relationship, and my half sister's motives make my whole body feel electric, as if it's being powered by confusion.

Even though I want all the bad feelings to disperse, when I pull into the semicircle of the driveway, the last part of my crazy week comes crashing down. There, way too close for comfort on the front steps, are Alexa and Tate. She kisses his cheek. There's no Russ to diffuse their intimacy, no twins to make it just a friendly peck—just the two of them, peering at one another and then at some love note they're both holding. As soon as they see me watching them, Alexa waves as if nothing's out of order and Tate shoves the piece of paper in his pocket.

The car ignition switches off, and my anger switches on. Every step I take on the pavement brings with it a piercing feeling of anxiety—my art is missing, my sister's hooking up with the guy I've liked for so long, and even if I never speak to Alexa again, she—or at least her gardening handi-work—is embedded in my backyard forever.

Alexa flops her arms onto my shoulders in an attempt to hug me, but I don't respond. Tate reaches out for my hand and I brush him off. I'm done being trampled on. "You guys are amazing, really." I point an accusatory finger at Tate. "You come out of nowhere and make me feel all these things, like that morning, in the back garden." I now point at Alexa. "The garden that *you* took over." I turn back to Tate. "I thought you were this great guy, but it turns out you're just a fake and a cheater."

Tate looks like I slapped him. "I'm not." Tate tries for my hand again, but I move away.

"You're wrong," Alexa says. "Whatever you think this is, it isn't."

Tate looks at Alexa, and I'm so tortured by their exchange of glances that I push past them and go inside. Alexa follows. "Jenny, wait. Let me explain."

I pivot and look at her. Tate remains on the front stoop, nervously shifting from one foot to the other. I'm sure he wishes he were on a field somewhere rather than here. "Fine. Then let me see the note Tate has."

Alexa's mouth is a perfect O of surprise, and yet she says, "What note?"

And just like that, all my suspicions are confirmed.

In the middle of all the tension, my mother comes in and begins sorting through the mail. "You kids all set for the carnival tomorrow?" she asks, oblivious to the fact that moments before I was ready to scream.

"I'm not sure I'm going," I say to her, and ignore Alexa.

216

"Oh, Jen. It's so fun! And Russ is going to be in the dunking booth. You know, youngest team member and everything."

The last thing I want right now is to be traipsing around the fairgrounds with sticky cotton candy hands and a gloomy heart, pretending to have a rocking old time while inside I feel betrayed. I imagine watching Tate with his sports buddies and feel sick.

"It's make your own pizza night!" Mom announces as if we should all clap our hands. "Who wants to help me make the dough right now?"

I shake my head. "No thanks." On the other side of the open door, Tate stands there, hands in his pockets, waiting for me to come out to him.

"I'll do it," Alexa says to my mother. "Let me just go and wash my hands."

I follow her into the half bathroom, invading her space like she's invaded mine. "So, is there anything else you want to say?"

Water runs from the faucet into the basin, and Alexa rubs the soap in her hands, looking at me in the mirror rather than face to face. "Like you said this morning, Jenny, there's nothing else to say. I can't explain anything to you right now. You've already decided that I'm guilty of something I didn't do."

"You know what?" I start to back out of the room. "You're right." I gaze at her mirrored self. She looks just like I did hours ago when I was crying. "You and I are done."

Chills and shakes rack my body as I leave her in the bathroom with the water still running and go back out to the entryway. Tate is gone.

Looks like he and I are done, too.

217

TWENTY-NINE

After Alexa charges past me in the hallway, I sit on the stairs in a slump, half furious and half defeated. How is it that everything I imagined she and I would share is so far from the truth? I glance upstairs and wonder if Alexa is brooding in my room or on the phone with Tate. I'm sick of wondering, tired of feeling left out. It seems crazy to me now that I thought Alexa could fill all the gaps in my life. Like people who have plastic surgery and suddenly expect things to be perfect. It isn't like that. Just like with my blank canvases, I'm the one who has to hold the brush, the one who has to make things happen. Only now with my paintings missing and Tate's disappearance, I realize that I'm going to have to start everything all over again.

From his study, Dad emerges decked out in his running gear. He puts his foot next to me on the stairs and ties his sneaker. I always watched him get ready to run when I was a kid. He'd check the weather, slide into shorts or sweats, or rain gear if necessary. He had been determined to move forward with his plan no matter what the elements had in store, and I'd feel as though I'd need much more than a Gore-Tex windbreaker to survive a run with him. I'd feel as though either way—if I ran with him or stayed behind—I'd wind up letting him down.

I shake my head at myself. Why do I make everything so complicated?

"What's up?" Dad asks as he double-knots his other shoelaces.

"Want some company?" I ask him. The surprise registers right away, but he manages a nod. I run upstairs and change my clothes faster than I ever have just in case I back out—or he does.

I join him as he stretches in the driveway, and then we're off.

"To what do I owe this honor?" Dad says, leading us around Mill's Pond and over the road on his usual loop through our suburban enclave.

"Just a change of pace," I say, not wanting to let him know I ran before with Tate. I want this to be special to him. "Hey, how about taking a detour into the woods?" Dad questions me with a look. "I know you like your routine, but—"

"Lead the way," he says.

My body feels the same way it did the other day while jogging with Tate—free, released, and fluid. But I'm also wishing that my dad will sense my inner frenzy and offer to make it all better. It's just a dream, but I still hold tight, like gripping a paintbrush.

"A couple of miles, maybe? Down the grassy path?" he asks.

"And then through the woods," I add. "Blah. I sound like a Christmas carol."

Dad smirks. "Nothing wrong with sounding quaint. Then again, it's probably not your style."

We keep running, with him kindly slowing down a bit so I can keep up. The street winds into the grassy path, behind houses with barbecues, lawns, and swing sets. "What is my style, exactly?" It's not that I want to test him, I just want to see what he knows about me. Okay, maybe I'm testing him a little.

"Hmmm . . ." Dad's shoes hit the grass softly, landing on the worn path where countless runs have taken place in the dusk. I feel glad to join their shadowy ranks. "I think you're the person who can describe it best. And I'm not saying that to avoid the question. It's just that I don't want to define you."

I breathe hard, heat gathering at my hairline and flushing my cheeks, and let Dad's words sink in. All this time I've been thinking that's exactly what he and the rest of my family have been doing—trying to define me. There's one way to find out if he means what he says.

We come to the road and Dad jogs in place as a car goes by. He looks at me and takes my hand, the way he did when I was five and wanted to pick dandelions across the road. We cross and then start up the incline and into the shade of pines and evergreens. And then I go for broke.

"Dad?" I stop and pretend to tie my shoe while sucking in air.

"Yeah?" He jogs in place, the dark cool of the woods in

the background. The edges of the trees look painted to me, all wavy lines of green and brown, like a van Gogh.

"How come you got rid of those watercolors I did in Montana?" Dad looks at me like I imagined them. "You know, the three-piece series." I make an outline in the air with my finger to show the rectangular shape.

"Oh, those?" Dad brushes his thinning hair away from his forehead. He sighs and puts his hands on his hips. He probably trashed them when we got back from the trip, or threw them away during one of the attic cleanup sessions.

"It's just that they're not at the house," I say, and stand up. "If you got rid of them—"

Dad cuts me off. "Of course I didn't. They're at my work office. I had them framed when we got back, and that took a few weeks, and then I brought them over." He looks at me. "What? People like looking at peaceful images when they're stressed, which they often are at mediation meetings."

I smile and shake my head in awe.

"What'd you think happened to them?" Dad asks. Then, as he watches my face, he gets it. "Oh, Jen, I'd never . . . Look, those are the first paintings you've ever given me."

"And?" I want to tell him what I need to hear, but there's only so much talking I can do.

"And I love them," he says. Wind sweeps through the pines, scenting the air just enough to make me think of fall and even further to winter. I know my father well enough, I realize, to understand he's not only talking about the paintings.

"So why didn't you tell me?" I start off on the path slowly now and he follows.

He pauses and thinks for a moment. "Maybe I was afraid you'd think I was trying too hard. Or worse, that you wouldn't believe me."

"Why wouldn't I?"

Dad wipes the sweat from his upper lip. "Because of all the pressure we put on you with the sports thing." He looks at me from the side. "I didn't want you think that any compliments were an attempt to—"

"Con me?"

"Right." Dad's feet pound the dirt path as he nods.

We run without saying anything for a while, dodging a few branches. I slip once on some rust-colored pine needles, but I don't let the fall bring me down. Near the end of the run as we circle back toward the grassy path, Dad brings up Alexa and her visit. He doesn't know about the Tate trouble, but maybe he suspects.

"So having Alexa here isn't quite what you expected?" Dad guesses.

The endorphin release from the exercise is similar to the one I get when I finish a painting, and for the first time I actually get why people do this regularly. "Not really."

"That's what I was afraid of." As soon as he says this, he trips on a tree root. "Damn!" He stops and grabs his ankle, wincing in pain. I rush over to him.

"Are you okay?"

He shakes his head. "No." He uses my shoulders for support and limps as I try to help him take the weight off his foot.

"I just need to rest for a while," he says, pointing to a tree stump. He hobbles over and sits down on it. I squat down in front of him and look at him with concern. "I'll be fine, really. I probably just sprained it."

"Dad?" I say, gazing into his eyes. "What were you *really* afraid of when you found out about Alexa?"

Dad keeps looking forward. "I was there for your birth, Jenny. I helped Mom when she threw up every day all the way through the last trimester with you. But knowing that someone else created you and that you'd found someone who shared that connection, I don't know. I felt so . . ."

"Insecure?" I say, thinking back to my argument with Alexa and what she said about Tate and me.

"Yes, definitely. I'd been feeling so detached from you lately, and when this happened, it just intensified."

My feet on the grass-soft ground feel heavy, my muscles sore. Dad gets up, and when he walks, has a full-on limp. I stand up and start walking next to him. We're pretty much silent until we get home. I'm thankful for my dad's honesty, and glad I asked him these questions. But there's still so much more to say.

When we get back to the house, Dad grabs a hiking pole from the boot room in the garage and uses it for balance. I line his sneakers up next to mine. We look at our feet next to one another's.

I breathe hard, still out of breath from the jog, the damp air filling my lungs and just as quickly emptying. Right now everything that's happened today is in the back of my mind, and only one thought is pushing to get out, so I let it go.

"Dad, all my life I felt like I was missing something. I

hope you don't take that the wrong way." I sneak a look at him, but Dad's still facing straight ahead. "Sometimes I'd look for my shoes and make sure I had them both on, or that I hadn't left my pajamas on, or misplaced that bracelet I never take off."

"The one I gave Mom when we first met?" Dad asks. His ankle is swelling, his sock white against the bruise.

I nod. "Yeah. But then, it wasn't a physical thing missing. Like how you don't know you need both your ankles until one—"

"Gets sprained?"

I nod. I think back to when my sibling search started—Tate showing me the article about the registry, how I debated logging on to the site, clicking on a message board posting, and finding her. That was just over a week ago. How is it possible to feel like I'm losing her already? "When I found out about the Donor Sibling Registry, it was as if I could have that missing part delivered to me."

"Via FedEx, apparently," Dad says. We both laugh. The shadows from the late-day light cast speckled sunlight onto my sneakers. "So even though we all act like it doesn't make a difference, it does, doesn't it?"

I get chills over my hot arms and look my dad straight in the eyes. "A little. I mean, you're my dad, right? You have been and always will be. But sometimes I just wish I had a part of you. Like how Sierra and Sage have your nose, and Russ has your throwing arm."

"But, Jenny, you're more like me than anyone else in the family," Dad says.

"I am?" I can't help but look at him as if he just

announced he was from another planet. A planet where I magically have his genes.

Dad sits down on the front porch, one long arm up into the sky, the other behind his back. "I never thought about it much before all this." He sweeps his hands between us as if the gesture will convey everything that's happened in the past couple of weeks. "But you are."

"How?" I pull my hair out of its elastic, feeling the sweat on my scalp. The wind feels so good on my head and face.

"We're both stubborn as hell." Dad smirks and pats me on the head. "We don't like surprises, and probably over-think to a fault. And we're both artists, except I facilitate words instead of colors."

When he says this, I actually feel fragments of gloom leave my chest, my heart lightens, and the smile comes out before I can curb it. "I like that. It kind of reminds me of that song—the one about van Gogh."

" 'Starry, Starry Night'?" Dad nods at me. "I sang that to you when you were a baby."

"I guess it worked," I say.

I help him up, and we walk into the house in a jumbled heap, moving like one solid mass. "Jen, if you want to see difference, you always will." He's probably said this to countless clients over the years, but it makes sense.

"And if you want to see similarities?" I ask.

"You can find those, too."

THIRTY

The next morning, I wake up late, wondering if I should give Alexa yet another chance. That's what mature people do, after all, right? Besides, it's just a giant drain on my psyche to have the weight of an argument on me. But then doubt lurches at me—when I think about her with Tate, the way she would casually touch his arm or look at him with her sleepy gaze, or how they always seem to be whispering, I feel ill. I'd like to think that a real sister wouldn't go after my semiboyfriend, but maybe that's what I get for jumping into this all so fast—on both fronts.

I sit up with my sheets pulled close to my chin, and what hits me first is how neat the room is. No piles of clothes, no wet bathing suits, no uneven blinds. And most important, no Alexa. I don't panic at first, but after searching the bathroom, calling for her, and finding her suitcase gone, I start to freak out.

It's as if I'm back at Downtown Studios, finding out that my paintings have gone missing. Which reminds me that I still haven't figured out where they are.

I shout up the attic stairs. "Alexa?"

"She's not here!" Russ yells.

I scramble down the stairs and find a note posted to the refrigerator underneath a strawberry-shaped magnet:

JF—

As fast as it started, it has to stop. At least for now. I'm taking a cab to the station. I'm sorry you got the wrong idea about me—about every-thing. Good luck with the show, and know that I'll be thinking of you.

AMC

I sit down at the kitchen table and read the words, and suddenly the world feels very small. The morning air is cool coming in through the kitchen window. We've lost summer suddenly, and Alexa is gone without even a good-bye.

My mom comes up next to me and gives me a pat on the head, like Dad did last night. I show her the note as my lower lip trembles and my eyes fill with tears.

"I get the feeling you don't want to tell me what happened," Mom says with her eyebrows raised. She totally wants to know, but I don't want to tangle her up in the drama. When I don't respond, Mom changes the subject. "Your phone's been buzzing since last night."

"I didn't know I left it down here," I say, sniffling. I get up and swipe my phone from the mail table while Mom takes her keys from the blue ceramic bowl and goes outside. I dial into voice mail, assuming it'll be Alexa with an apology. Or Tate with a heart as heavy as mine is.

"Hello, Jenny. I'm Jamaica Haas. I'm sorry, but . . ." There's a pause and the sound of papers shuffling in the background. Maybe she has some information on my paintings. "Sid Sleethly no longer works here. We've had to let him go. And as a result, I've stepped in as director of the art showcase."

My heart sinks. If my paintings hadn't gone MIA, I would have had a shot with Jamaica in charge. I listen to the remainder of the message. "The good news is that one of your paintings turned up, and we'd like to put it on display for the show. Please give me a call at the following number and let us know the title for your piece. Thanks, and congratulations!"

My emotions go from bottom-rolling to top-of-the-heap jumping. Not only am I relieved that someone found one of my paintings, but I am so excited about the show that I shout to anyone who'll listen in my house. "I'm in! I'm in the art show! It's official!" And Sid Sleethly is out of my life for good!

I scream it, but no one yells back. Wasn't Russ just upstairs? And my mother down in the hallway? Despite slightly improved family relations, I feel suspiciously like no one cares. Then I think if Alexa were here, she would, but she's not, because of me.

With my brain on overload, Dad decides now's the time to reshoot the family portrait.

"Everyone in a huddle," he commands from his perch on

228

the patio wall. The photographer is ready to go. I slink outside with my stained purple shirt, bunched up in front, trying to hide the paint streaks. Of course, Sierra and Sage's tiny tees are perfect, Russ's might have a wrinkle or two but is basically fine, and Mom looks like she's on the cover of a department store catalog.

"Jenny?" Mom waves me over and I stand next to her. Dad looks down at me, noticing how I've rolled my shirt into a mush.

"Straighten it out, Jen."

"It's fine the way it is," I say. *Same old, same old,* is what I think. Then Dad jumps down from the wall and pulls the shirt down so it hangs once again past my waist.

"Not the best fit, eh?" He studies it. I watch his face change when he sees the paint marks.

"Yeah, it's kind of big," I reply.

"Maybe in my mind you're taller or something," he says. His voice is gentle, not angry like I thought it would be. "I see you took it upon yourself to decorate the shirt." He sighs.

I shrug. "Sorry, I didn't mean to. I just thought we were done with it."

"It's better than that twisty thing you had going on before," Russ says, grinning.

"Now you just look like you," Sierra adds. It's not mean, just honest. And she's correct. I turn to face the camera, giving a normal, not overdone, smile.

"Ready?" The photographer clicks away, capturing us in the moment.

Yes, I think. *I am.*

But for what, I'm still not sure.

The town center is jammed with cars, all vying for a space close to the high school. Carnival Day is a townwide event. I'm still planning on going, even though I haven't seen or heard from Tate in a bit and it feels weird knowing our "relationship" might be over because of what happened with Alexa. I tried calling her, tried calling her mothers' phone, but got no answer. If it weren't for the art show, I would have locked myself in my room for a few days until Faye came back, but at least there is something to look forward to and take pride in, regardless of all the losses I've had.

I weave through people doing back-to-school shopping and head toward Downtown. Relieved that I won't have to deal with Sid, I find the back door locked, not propped open as it usually is, and have to go around to the front. Inside, the calmness takes over and I feel a sense of homecoming. Even better than that, actually, because Sid is no longer here, although I'm dying to know why.

"What do you think?" Jamaica is dressed all in violet and standing in the doorway. "You're on this wall."

Nerves and excitement bristle up and down my arms and spine. I turn and see the orange painting with overlapping circles, each one blending into the next. The unfinished edges draw attention to the painting, even though it's not the biggest one out there, not by a long shot. Still, I feel as though I have accomplished something huge. "I love it!" I go over and shake her hand enthusiastically. "Thank you so much!"

"It's a pleasure," she says. "Now, if you can tell me what you'd like to call it. Sid had the list of titles, you see, and, well, he was asked to leave rather quickly." She gives me a look. "Conflict of personalities. I'm sure you understand."

I nod to tell her that of course I get it—who didn't conflict with Sid? But suddenly I realize that my other paintings are still nowhere to be found. "Have you seen any other paintings of mine?" My brow tightens and my throat becomes dry. "They look similar to this one, with unfinished edges."

Jamaica shakes her head. "No. I'm sorry, I haven't. Sid left this here, leaning on the wall, which meant we were to include it in the show."

"You mean, he liked it?" I can't fight my smile. I figured he thought it was horrible.

"Yes, yes he did. . . . For all his pretensions, he got this right. He liked it—and so do I."

She doesn't elaborate on what happened to Sid and where he's gone, but waits for me to give her a title. I think with my hands resting on my hips while I stare at the painting. It shouldn't be hard to name something, should it? I think hard about Alexa, her sleepy gaze, how much I wanted her to be my own twin, and how part of that was just a cover for wanting to feel attached and important to my own life.

"I know," I say to Jamaica. She has her pen poised on the clipboard and waits for my answer. A feeling of peace settles into the already full palette of my life, and thoughts of new beginnings start. *"The Other Half of Me."*

She nods. "Great fit."

By the high school, the tall circle of the Ferris wheel is visible from far away. Last year, and all the years before, I ran into the carnival searching for cotton candy, soaking up the smells of fried dough, bumping into people from school, feeling like a tiny dot amid a huge splattering of colors and faces. This year I decide to forgo the actual games and rides for a while and take a seat on the sun-warmed bleachers. The pinpricks of anticipation for the show are constant, as is a sense of exhilaration from making it in.

From a distance the sway of the pirate ship ride; the crazy whirl of the Loop; the shrieks from kids; the cheerleaders with too much makeup, their hair in high ponytails—it all seems harmonious. I can almost allow myself to forget that somewhere in that mass of sights and sounds Tate is chucking pies at people or winning cute girls in color-coordinated outfits prizes of fluffy snakes. Or maybe Tate isn't there, but at home and online with Alexa. Maybe they've officially paired off. The thought makes me so crazed I want to scream, but instead I tilt my face to the sky and admit I just need to find him and confront him.

The steps behind me rattle with footsteps. It's funny, I realize, to even be sitting here in the sports zone. It's not my typical place during the school year. Then again, who knows what this year will bring.

A tap on my shoulder produces a heavenly hot Tate in a

plain gray T-shirt, green shorts, a wide grin, and penetrating eyes that make me instantly aware of how much I liked him—still like him—no matter what happened with him and Alexa. But I won't be *that* girl, the one who gets cheated on and sucks it up.

"I got you this," he says, and holds out a Sno-Kone. "I thought you'd like the colors." I accept the offering and look at the mound of crushed ice—swirls of red, yellow, and blue wash across the top, and I put it to my mouth, enjoying the sweetness and glad that it hides my lips, just in case they give away how much I want him to kiss me. Then I banish the thought.

"Thanks. Don't you want one?"

Tate shakes his head. He stands with his back to the sun, so his hair looks golden-edged, his skin glowing. "Nah, that's okay. I can share yours, right?" He looks at me, wondering.

"Sure." I take a cold bite and hand it to him. Then I come right out with it. "So, you know Alexa's gone, right?" I figure his reaction to this news will show how much she means to him—either he won't mind or he'll be hurt.

Tate's hand freezes on its way to his mouth. The Sno-Kone drips there in midair. "She's what?" His voice says it all—he's upset.

"Gone," I say. "As in, she vacated and took the train back into the city."

"But, she and I . . ." He stops himself. Hearing the two of them paired by his words makes me crumble inside. He likes her. I feel as though I will always be that girl who is cast aside, the one in the corner, painting the scene rather

233

than being in it. "Why? What happened?" He offers the cone back to me and I shake my head.

"Oh, I think we both know what happened." I look at him and back at the fairgrounds. Two days from now, the art show will be finished, the Ferris wheel deconstructed, and school back in session. That so-called magic of summer will evaporate.

"Oh," Tate says, and licks the cone again. "So you know, then?"

Fury runs through me. "So it's true?" I bark.

Tate looks confused. "Whoa, wait a sec. What are *you* talking about?"

I stomp my foot on the metal steps and the sound registers louder than I meant it to. "You and Alexa. Together!"

Tate talks fast. "No, no, no. You're wrong, Fitz. How could you think that I . . ." He points to his chest. A chest I hugged. Who knows what Alexa did to it? "Hooked up with Alexa?"

His words surprise me. Here I thought he had the perfect breakup scenario: carnival, friends waiting for him by the balloon arcade, Sno-Kone as consolation prize, and a clean break before school starts. "You didn't?" My eyebrows are raised so high they practically touch my scalp.

"No way! She's your sister. Why would I do that to you?"

"I know, but you guys were always whispering, and talking, and you called her or she called you or whatever, and it was like . . ."

Tate looks at me and then sits down next to me. "Like we had a secret?"

234

It's my turn to stand up. "Yes. Exactly." When something big is about to happen, everything appears clearer—the sky bright blue, the outlines of objects crisp, each word vivid.

"Well, we did." Tate looks up at me, his legs stretched out enough that if I were to move one inch to the left I'd touch his calf. "We still do."

I don't do him the favor of sticking around. I don't need him to tell me what I already know. I move quickly down the bleachers, sure that Tate will follow—isn't that the way it always is in movies? The guy chasing after the girl to tell her the truth? To say he still cares about her? But when I look back, Tate isn't even there—he's running down the other side of the steps and disappearing into the polka-dot crowd of the carnival.

THIRTY-ONE

My linen dress is cut close enough that I'm not swallowed by fabric, as Sierra and Sage once told me in reference to my baggy T-shirts, but not so close I'm self-conscious. And for once, I'm paint-free. Except the twins aren't here to see for themselves, nor is the rest of my family.

Just when I thought everything was on the slow climb upward, I find myself at the art show, program in hand, and alone. Well, not completely alone. My parents slipped a card into my bag saying congratulations, and Russ left a note on my dashboard saying good luck. The twins left overlapping messages on my cell phone. But it's not the same as having them here with me.

Of course, I blame myself a little. I was the one who shrugged off the show, who told them to go and see Sierra and Sage's performance. The one thing keeping me going is that my art is finally on view for all to see. The seesaw of my emotions is making me off balance; I feel guilty that I'm missing out on the twins' performance (although I arranged for two bouquets of gerbera daisies to be delivered to their show), crumpled about Alexa and Tate, yet thrilled at being right here, right now.

People hold cups of chilled punch in their hands as they mingle and chat about the sculptures and paintings, and I watch them as much as I look at the art. It's a relief to be at the studios but free of Sid and his ever-present critiques. Jamaica Haas gives me a nod from across the room, and I fight the urge to go and check on my painting. Then I figure it's okay if I do, sort of like visiting an old friend. That's the thing about art: after you make it, it's not really yours any-more, more everyone else's.

I stand in front of it and remember each slash of color, each stroke of purple and orange, the wax I put in to delay the drying time. Tate once commented that my paintings are filled with circles, and I guess he's right. Now I realize the spheres are like family, everything joined together in teams. Maybe the point of art—and of everything—is that you can't predict the outcome, that the crazy upheaval of it all is part of life. The recall of that overwhelming anxiety I felt when I first clicked on Alexa's posting comes back when I think about not seeing her again.

"Well done, Jenny Fitzgerald."

I know right away who that pinched voice belongs to. Perhaps my relief was premature. "Hello, Sid," I say, and it sounds formal. Then again, I'm at an art show wearing a dress, so maybe I should be on my best behavior. "I thought you weren't—"

"Employed here anymore?" he asks, and purses his lips. He may as well have a sign around his neck reading ASK ME IF I'M ANNOYING. "Well, the rumors are true. I've given up this suburban existence and moved back into the city." He pauses and looks around at the crowd. "It's where everything important is happening."

He leaves out any notion of being fired—but maybe that's art, too, making up your own reality in order to get on with life. I think about Alexa's enthusiasm about me moving to the city, even if it was only for a semester, and how that would never have worked.

Sid points a finger at my painting. "So, it hasn't sold. Shame."

I look at the title card on the wall and see that it has no red dot like many of the other paintings. Red dot stickers signify that a painting has been sold, and a quick sweep of the room informs me that mine is one of the few that hasn't.

"You know what, though? I'm just so glad to have my painting here. I don't care if it sells. Who cares who buys what in art? I mean, the point is just to do it. To find what you want to say and say it!"

Part of what I said is true. Getting what you want feels good, but not the way it should if you're completely without people to share it with. Alone, I wait for Sid's pointed reply.

Instead of being obnoxious, he's very calm. "That's precisely what I was hoping you'd learn. Bravo!"

Even though Sid is evil incarnate and semistrange, it feels good to be praised by someone who knows what he's talking about. "Thanks, Sid." He raises a glass to toast me when I remember to ask him something. "By the way, have you seen the other paintings I did? The ones that kind of go with this one?"

His mouth goes back into twisted mode. "I have, actually. They're tucked away in the storage space upstairs. Ask Jamaica for the key." He pauses. "All except one—the rather bold blue?"

I make a face. "Whatdoyoumean?" My words come out so fast I sound like Sierra and Sage. "Where's that one?"

He points a finger at me, scolding. "Oh, relax. I took it into the city with me. How do I say this without filling your head with fluff?" He puts his hand dramatically on his forehead and pauses, just to drive me crazy. Then he continues. "Jamaica Haas thinks you've got talent. I respect her opinion, obviously, but not more than my own. After some consideration, this new direction of yours shows promise. Enough that I've put the blue one—temporarily, mind you—in my new gallery."

My mouth hangs open, and I have to tame the urge to jump up and down grade-school style. Excitement swirls around me and everything goes painty, with colors and swirls and blotches. But again, I'm at a loss—I have no hand to squeeze in sisterly excitement, no parental gaze to congratulate me. No Tate to swoop in for a kiss. "Really? In the city? A gallery? *My* work?"

"Do you realize you've just asked four incomplete questions?" Sid narrows his eyes. "We'll talk more later. I have to mingle." And with that, Sid Sleethly glides away to ogle other artwork. "And it's only by the bathroom at the gallery—don't be too overjoyed."

But I am. I stand with my painting, looking at the title card with no sticker, and wishing I had someone to share my good news with. And then, right when I think I'll break in two, I see him. Standing in the doorframe in a suit, looking like a piece of art himself, is Tate. He sees me notice him and comes over right away.

"Before you say anything, let me explain," he states, when I'm already contemplating the statute of limitations on apologies. "From the minute Alexa got here, she and I had . . . a thing." I feel like someone has dropped a slab of concrete on me. I want to tell him to stop—I can't hear it anymore—but he keeps going. "I tried so hard to keep it a secret from you, and I wish I hadn't. But Fitz, you're what I've been wishing for."

I've never been more confused.

"But what about—"

"Wait." Tate punctuates his word with a hand on my shoulder. "There wasn't anything between me and Alexa. We were just—"

Tate's reveal is interrupted by familiar faces all in a jumble by the buffet table. "There she is! Jenny!" Sierra and Sage, each carrying the flowers I sent them, come dashing over to me. Their faces are matte with stage makeup, but they smile at me while my parents follow behind.

"You're here!" I exclaim.

"Don't sound so shocked," Russ says as he joins us.

"You didn't think we'd really miss this, did you?" My dad comes over, still in a half limp from his twisted ankle. Despite the injury, he manages to hug me so hard he lifts me off the ground.

"Well," I say, "this is it. This is my painting." I'm about to explain what I tried to do and how, but I know now it doesn't matter, that they can see it however they want. The important thing is they're here with me.

"So we're too late, I see," Mom says and points to the title card. When she does, I realize she's been pointing that way my whole life; to the lopsided clay pots I glazed in second grade, to my first tries at "real" painting in seventh, to just plain old paint-streaked me. That to her, I am the art, and instead of feeling embarrassed or annoyed, I just smile.

"Cool name," Sierra says, and Sage nods. They, too, gesture to the red dot as though it's an on button.

I smirk. "You guys didn't have to do that," I say. "It's really fine with me if no one buys it."

I reach over and start to pick at the sticker with my fingernail. It's sweet that my family wants my work, but not necessary. I remember having my own art sale, how I roped a five-year-old Russ into playing the art dealer while I displayed my wares on the floor of the living room. Together, we sold a drawing I'd made of our family then, with me, Russ, our parents, and the twins as simple orbs, little babies without personalities. Now I'd like to try my hand at them again, at all of us, this fully formed group.

"We didn't buy it," Mom says. She clamps her lips over her teeth and shakes her head, trying to prove she's serious.

"We would have," Dad says. He puts his arm over my shoulder, and I can feel him lean just a little on me, his ankle still sore.

I look around, wondering what the deal is, and then I catch Jamaica's eye again. She points to the painting and then to me. So it wasn't my family, but an artist—a real, working, fellow artist who bought it. I smile and lean into the huddle of my family.

"So can we go?" Sierra asks. She's dressed differently from Sage, with her hair purposely parted on the other side. Even they've reached the point where being close doesn't mean having to be the same.

"Yeah," Sage says, "we should."

"That's it? You guys just pop in and then leave?"

"She doesn't know yet," Tate says. Then he puts both hands on my shoulders and turns me so I'm facing him. All gorgeous six feet of him. "There's a party for you at your house." Tate looks at my parents and they nod. "Alexa planned it and got us all involved. That's what all the whispering and secrets were about. She figured that even if you didn't make it into the show, you deserved some attention."

There's nothing like misunderstanding to make you feel like an idiot, but when I see the colorful tent in the backyard, all feelings of idiocy melt away. The only regret I have is that Alexa isn't here with me. I tried to call her from Downtown, but all I got was her voice mail.

From my familiar place by the window in my bedroom, I look out at the silver and gold star balloons, the pointed tent, and the amazing food. With my best friend Faye's help, Alexa enlisted the chef from her program to make famous paintings out of food. Van Gogh's *The Starry Night* is recreated in cupcakes, and Mondrian's *Broadway Boogie Woogie* is fashioned from imported cheese and artisan breads. Alexa outdid herself, which is why I ran up here.

Before I go out and join Tate and my family, the friends who have gathered in my honor, before I celebrate myself, I have to call her and say I'm sorry. While I put the program from the art show on my desk to savor later, I call her, but no one answers—not even voice mail. So I go to my computer and IM her, but nothing happens. Then I e-mail Alexa, hoping she'll understand what I mean when I say I can't lose her—and that I was wrong.

> *Alexa,*
> *A lot of painting techniques involve "broken color." You use one or more colors in choppy layers over a different base coat to create a stippled or textured effect—maybe this sounds way more complicated than I mean. What I'm trying to say, in my own broken way, is that I'm sorry. And I miss you. I know you didn't lie to me about Tate. The party is in full swing downstairs, and I wish you were here. I also want to thank you, because even though it sucked having things deteriorate while you were here, it's made my regular life a little better. I knew finding you would change my life— I guess I just didn't know it would change me. That's all for now. I hope there's more later.*
> *JF*

I could have added that everything's okay with Tate, though we haven't completely solidified what happens in the hallway on Tuesday at school, and I could tell her how much more a part of my regular family I feel, but I suspect she knows that. I press send and wait to hear back.

My room feels wider than it did when Alexa was here. Maybe I'm not as good at sharing my space as I thought I'd be, but it feels—or I feel—different. The newly done garden area is filled with draping white lights, calling attention to the space Alexa worked on with my dad. I was so upset then, but now as this has all unfolded, I'm glad to have her mark on this house. It's like a visual reminder of how she altered my life. Or helped me alter my own.

"Hey, Jenny," Russ knocks on my door.

"I know, I'm coming," I say, and stop hunching over my keyboard.

"Come here," he says, and I follow him out into the hallway to the attic door. "Go on up."

I give him the *you're crazy* look. "With the dead moths and boxes of fashion mistakes from years past? No thanks."

"Just go." Russ pushes me up the stairs to the dark attic. When I turn on the lights, I'm in awe: the once cluttered room is now pristine. Track lights shine onto two large tables, and trays of new art supplies are arranged in perfect symmetry at the far end of one of them.

"Oh my . . . ," I start, but my voice trails off as I wander around, touching everything as though I need to confirm its existence. "This is unreal!" I touch the easels, the canvas-stretching machine, and the creamy ceramic bowl that holds new brushes.

"It's pretty good, isn't it?" Russ smiles at me with his

winning game face—the expression I've only ever seen him have at all-star games and MVP announcements.

"Thank you, Russ." I hug him and repeat myself until he pushes me away.

"We all thought you deserved it." He goes to the wall and flips a switch. "And the best part?"

"What?" Then I get it. "Ventilation!"

Russ nods. "Only clean air from now on."

"This is incredible. I have to go thank everyone," I say.

"Yeah, we should get to the party," Russ says. "But, um, maybe you should change your dress?"

"Why?" I look down and expect to see my clean linen-ed self, but instead find that I've somehow managed to back into some wet paint and my backside is graced with a smear of orange paint. "You know what? I just am who I am." I laugh. "You can only change so much, right?"

Russ goes out to join the festivities, and I dart back into my room to get my camera. I want to remember everything about this night. I turn off the lights in my bedroom and am about to head into the party when I see my computer blinking at me.

I walk to the screen and peek outside again. If it weren't for Alexa, none of this would have happened—not just the party, but all of it. I feel tethered to everyone outside, and to Alexa, wherever she is. Maybe that's the best kind of family, always there but not smothering you. I move the mouse over the blinking message on the screen while noises from the party filter up to my window from outside. Tate sees me in the window and waves, and I feel a rush.

Jenny—

I see that it's a message from Alexa and my heart pivots.

Sorry sorry sorry. We're both sorry. I know you called but I didn't pick up—

Again my stomach dips as I read—what if she never wants to talk again?

I'm sure you have a lot to say, but so do I. I didn't call, because I was mad and hurt. Still, there's something you need to know.

I swallow and prepare myself for what's next.

As soon as I got home, I had an e-mail waiting for me.

I hear my parents calling for me from outside. I hear Tate laughing and my sisters singing some song. I wonder about the future, about seeing Alexa in the city and checking on my artwork there, about running with my dad and about fall and school and if Tate will hold my hand as we walk through the school doors. I keep reading Alexa's message, wondering what she thinks I need to know.

You and I are sisters, right? I think we've proven that. But this e-mail I got—well, it changes things. What I'm try-ing to tell you is that there's someone else—another one of us. A sibling connected through Donor 142.

I don't have to reared the message to absorb all the content. More of us. Us.

Just when you think you have summed everything up, painted it clearly and given meaning to what was once just a pool of colored paint, another canvas crops up blank and ready to be filled. Another one of us. Expectations are only half of what you can imagine—one part what you want, another part what you only think you do. So I never had my perfect fit with Alexa, and I didn't get that Ferris wheel with Tate, yet there are other moments I've had in the past two weeks I couldn't have envisioned. Maybe that's what the best part of life is, those days or minutes you can't ever frame or paint beforehand.

After I e-mail her back, I make my way out to the backyard. I am part of a circle of family and friends. Music hums from the large speakers, the path to the tent is torchlighted, and everywhere laughter and talking meshes to form a backdrop of contenment. Yes, fall is days away, change imminent, but for right now, I am here.

There are circles everywhere; twenty-four-hour days and cycles, drawings of full moons and suns made by kids across the globe. The point is that the days and circles keep coming if you're lucky. Events matter, whether they are marble-small and ordinary, or the enormous ones that stretch out oceanwide. Each moment pulls you from the past into now, and then into whatever is next on your horizon.

ABOUT THE AUTHOR

Emily Franklin is the author of the critically acclaimed series The Principles of Love, as well as two novels for adults, *The Girls' Almanac* and *Liner Notes*. Forthcoming from Penguin is another series, Chalet Girls. Emily Franklin edited the anthology *It's a Wonderful Lie: 26 Truths About Life in Your Twenties* and the forthcoming essay collection *How Do You Spell Chanukah?* She is the coeditor of *Before: Short Stories About Pregnancy from Our Top Writers.* Her work has appeared in the *Boston Globe* and *Mississippi Review,* as well as in *Some Kind of Wonderful: Contemporary Writers on the Films of John Hughes* and *When I Was a Loser: True Stories of (Barely) Surviving High School.* Emily Franklin lives near Boston with her husband and their young children.